Bert Wilson, Wireless Operator

By

J. W. Duffield

BERT WILSON, WIRELESS OPERATOR

CHAPTER I

RUNNING AMUCK

"Amuck! Amuck! He's running amuck! Quick! For your lives!"

The drowsy water front pulsed into sudden life. There was a sound of running feet, of hoarse yells, a shriek of pain and terror as a knife bit into flesh, and a lithe, brown figure leaped upon the steamer's rail.

It was a frightful picture he presented, as he stood there, holding to a stanchion with one hand, while, in the other, he held a crooked dagger whose point was stained an ominous red. He was small and wiry, only a little over five feet in height, but strong and quick as a panther. His black hair, glossy with cocoa oil, streamed in the wind, his eyes were lurid with the wild light of insanity, his lips were parted in a savage snarl, and he was foaming at the mouth. He had lost all semblance of humanity, and as he stood there looking for another victim, he might have been transported bodily from one of Doré's pictures of Dante's Inferno. Suddenly, he caught sight of a group of three coming down the pier, and leaping to the wharf, he started toward them, his bare feet padding along noiselessly, while he tightened his grip on the murderous knife. A shot rang out behind him but missed him, and he kept on steadily, drawing nearer and nearer to his intended prey.

The three companions, toward whom doom was coming so swiftly and fearfully, were now halfway down the pier. They were typical young Americans, tall, clean cut, well knit, and with that easy swing and carriage that marks the athlete and bespeaks splendid physical condition. They had been laughing and jesting and were evidently on excellent terms with life. Their eyes were bright, their faces tinged with the bronzed red of perfect health, the blood ran warmly through their veins, and it seemed a bitter jest of fate that over them, of all men, should be flung the sinister shadow of death. Yet never in all their life had they been so near to it as on that sleepy summer afternoon on that San Francisco wharf.

At the sound of the shot they looked up curiously. And then they saw.

By this time the Malay was not more than fifty feet away. He was running as a mad dog runs, his head shaking from side to side, his kriss brandished aloft, his burning eyes fixed on the central figure of the three. He expected to die, was eager to die, but first he wanted to kill. The dreadful madness peculiar to the Malay race had come upon him, and the savage instincts that slumbered in him were now at flood. He had made all his preparations for death, had prayed to his deities, blackened his teeth as a sign of his intention, and devoted himself to the infernal gods. Then by the use of maddening drugs he had worked himself into a state of wild delirium and started forth to slay. They had sought to stop him as he rushed out from the cook's galley, but he had slashed wildly right and left and one of them had been left dangerously wounded on the steamer's deck. The captain and mates had rushed to their cabins to get their revolvers, and it was the shot from one of these that had tried vainly to halt him in his death dealing course. The crew, unarmed, had sought refuge where they could, and now, with his thirst for blood still unslaked, he rushed toward the unsuspecting strangers.

For one awful instant their hearts stood still as they caught sight of the fiendish figure bearing down upon them. None of them had a weapon. They had never dreamed of needing one. Their stout hearts and, at need, their fists, had always proved sufficient, and they shared the healthy American repugnance at relying on anything else than nature had given them. There was no way to evade the issue. Had they turned, the madman, with the impetus he already had, would have been upon them before they could get under way. There was no alternative. They must play with that grim gambler, Death, with their lives as the stakes. And at the thought, they stiffened.

The Malay was within ten feet. Quick as a flash, the taller of the three dove straight for the madman's legs. The latter made a wicked slash downward, but his arm was caught in a grip of iron, and the next instant the would-be murderer was thrown headlong to the pier, his knife clattering harmlessly to one side. The three were on him at once, and, though he fought like a wildcat, they held him until the crowd, bold now that the danger was past, swarmed down on the wharf and trussed him securely with ropes. Then the trio rose, shook themselves and looked at each other.

"By Jove, Bert," said the one who had grasped the Malay's arm as it was upraised to strike, "that was the dandiest tackle I ever saw, and I've seen you make a good many. If you'd done that in a football game on Thanksgiving day, they'd talk of it from one end of the country to the other."

"O, I don't know, Dick," responded Bert. "Perhaps it wasn't so bad, but then, you know, I never had so much at stake before. Even at that I guess it would have been all up with me, if you hadn't grabbed that fellow's hand just at the minute you did."

"If I hadn't, Tom would," rejoined Dick lightly. "He went for it at the same instant, but I was on the side of the knife hand and so got there first. But it was a fearfully close shave," he went on soberly, "and I for one have had enough of crazy Malays to last me a lifetime."

"Amen to that," chimed in Tom, fervently, "a little of that sort of thing goes a great way. If this is a sample of what we're going to meet, there won't be much monotony on this trip."

"Well, no," laughed Bert, "not so that you could notice it. Still, when you tackle the Pacific Ocean, you're going to find it a different proposition from sailing on a mill pond, and I shouldn't be surprised if we found action enough to keep our joints from getting rusty before we get back."

The crowd that had seemed to come from everywhere were loud in their commendation of the boys' courage and presence of mind. Soon, an ambulance that had been hastily summoned rattled up to the pier, at top speed, and took charge of the wounded sailor, while a patrol wagon carried the maniac to the city prison. The throng melted away as rapidly as it had gathered, and the three chums mounted the gangway of the steamer. A tall, broad shouldered man in a captain's uniform advanced to greet them.

"That was one of the pluckiest things I ever saw," he said warmly, as he grasped their hands. "You were lucky to come out of that scrape alive. Those Malays are holy terrors when they once get started. I've seen them running amuck in Singapore and Penang before now, but never yet on this side of the big pond. That fellow has been sullen and moody for days, but I've been so busy getting ready to sail that I didn't give it a second thought. I had a bead drawn on the beggar when he was making toward you, but didn't dare to fire for fear of hitting one of you. But all's well that ends well, and I'm glad you came through it without a scratch. You were coming toward the ship," he went on, as he looked at them inquiringly, "and I take it that your business was with me."

"Yes, sir," answered Bert, acting as spokesman. "My name is Wilson, and these are my two friends, Mr. Trent and Mr. Henderson."

"Wilson," repeated the captain in pleased surprise. "Why, not the wireless operator that the company told me they had engaged to make this trip?"

"The same," replied Bert, smiling.

"Well, well," said the captain, "I'm doubly glad to meet you, although I had no idea that our first meeting would take place under such exciting circumstances. You can't complain that we didn't give you a warm reception," he laughed. "Come along, and I'll show you your quarters and introduce you to the other officers."

Had any one told Bert Wilson, a month earlier, that on this June day he would be the wireless operator of the good ship "Fearless," Abel Manning, Captain, engaged in the China trade, he would have regarded it as a joke or a dream. He had just finished his Freshman year in College. It had been a momentous year for him in more ways than one. He had won distinction in his studies—a matter of some satisfaction to his teachers. But he had been still more prominent on the college diamond—a matter of more satisfaction to his fellow students. He had just emerged from a heart breaking contest, in which his masterly twirling had won the pennant for his Alma Mater, and incidentally placed him in the very front rank of college pitchers. His plans for the summer vacation were slowly taking shape, when, one day, he was summoned to the office of the Dean.

"Sit down, Wilson," he said, as he looked up from some papers, "I'll be at liberty in a moment."

For a few minutes he wrote busily, and then whirled about in his office chair and faced Bert, pleasantly.

"What are your plans for the summer, Wilson?" he asked. "Have you anything definite as yet?"

"Not exactly, sir," answered Bert. "I've had several invitations to spend part of the time with friends, but, as perhaps you know, I haven't any too much money, and I want to earn some during the vacation, to help me cover my expenses for next year. I've written to my Congressman at Washington to try to get me work in one of the wireless stations on the coast, but there seems to be so much delay and red tape about it that I don't know whether it will amount to anything. If that doesn't develop, I'll try something else."

"Hum," said the Dean, as he turned to his desk and took a letter from a pigeon hole. "Now I have here a line from Mr. Quinby, the manager of a big fleet of steamers plying between San Francisco and the chief ports of China. It seems that one of his vessels, the Fearless, needs a good wireless operator. The last one was careless and incompetent, and the line had to let him go. Mr. Quinby is an old grad of the college, and an intimate personal friend of mine. He knows the thoroughness of our scientific course"—here a note of pride crept into the Dean's voice—"and he writes to know if I can recommend one of our boys for the place. The voyage will take between two and three months, so that you can be back by the time that college opens in the Fall. The pay is good and you will have a chance to see something of the world. How would you like the position?"

How would he like it? Bert's head was in a whirl. He had always wanted to travel, but it had seemed like an "iridescent dream," to be realized, if at all, in the far distant future. Now it was suddenly made a splendid possibility. China and the islands of the sea, the lands of fruits and flowers, of lotus and palm, of minarets and pagodas, of glorious dawns and glittering noons and spangled nights! The East rose before him, with its inscrutable wisdom, its passionless repose, its heavy-lidded calm. It lured him with its potency and mystery, its witchery and beauty. Would he go!

He roused himself with an effort and saw the Dean regarding him with a quizzical smile.

"Like it," he said enthusiastically, "there's nothing in all the world I should like so well. That is," he added, "if you are sure I can do the work. You know of course that I've had no practical experience."

"Yes," said the Dean, "but I've already had a talk with your Professor of Applied Electricity, and he says that there isn't a thing about wireless telegraphy that you don't understand. He tells me that you are equally familiar with the Morse and the Continental codes, and that you are quicker to detect and remedy a defect than any boy in your class. From theory to practice will not be far, and he is confident that before your ship clears the Golden Gate you'll know every secret of its wireless equipment from A to Z. I don't mind telling you that your name was the first one that occurred to both him and myself, as soon as the matter was broached. Mr. Quinby has left the whole thing to me, so that, if you wish to go, we'll consider the matter settled, and I'll send him a wire at once."

"I'll go," said Bert, "and glad of the chance. I can't thank you enough for your kindness and confidence, but I'll do my very best to deserve it."

"I'm sure of that," was the genial response, and, after a few more details of time and place had been settled, Bert took the extended hand of the Dean and left the office, feeling as though he were walking on air.

His first impulse was to hunt up his two chums, Tom and Dick, and tell them of his good fortune. Tom was a fellow classmate, while Dick had had one year more of college life. The bond that united them was no common one, and had been cemented by a number of experiences shared together for several years back. More than once they had faced serious injury or possible death together, in their many scrapes and adventures, and the way they had backed each other up had convinced each that he had in the others comrades staunch and true. During the present year, they had all been members of the baseball team, Tom holding down third base in dashing style and Dick starring at first; and many a time the three had pulled games out of the fire and wrested victory from defeat. In work and fun they were inseparable; and straight to them now Bert went, flushed and elated with the good luck that had befallen him.

"Bully for you, old man," shouted Dick, while Tom grabbed his hand and clapped him on the back; "It's the finest thing that ever happened."

"It sure is," echoed Tom. "Just think of good old Bert among the Chinks. And the tea houses—and the tomtoms—and the bazaars—and the jinrikishas—and all the rest. By the time he gets back, he'll have almond eyes and a pig-tail and be eating his rice with chop sticks."

"Not quite as bad as that, I hope," laughed Bert. "I've no ambition to be anything else than a good American, and probably all I'll see abroad will only make me the more glad to see the Stars and Stripes again when I get back to 'God's country.' But it surely will be some experience."

Now that the first excitement was over, the conversation lagged a little, and a slight sense of constraint fell upon them. All were thinking of the same thing. Tom was the first to voice the common thought.

"Gee, Bert," he said, "how I wish that Dick and I were coming along!"

"Why not?" asked Dick, calmly.

Bert and Tom looked at him in amazement.

"What!" yelled Bert. "You don't really think there's a chance?"

"A chance? Yes," answered Dick. "Of course it's nothing but a chance — as yet. The whole thing is so sudden and there are so many things to be taken into account that it can't be doped out all at once. It may prove only a pipe dream after all. But Father promised me a trip abroad at the end of my course, if I got through all right, and, under the circumstances, he may be willing to anticipate a little. Then too, you know, he's a red-hot baseball fan, and he's tickled to death at the way we trimmed the other teams this year. And we all know that Tom's folks have money to burn, and it ought to be no trick at all for him to get their consent. I tell you what, fellows, let's get busy with the home people, right on the jump."

And get busy they did, with the result that after a great deal of humming and hawing and backing and filling, the longed for consents were more or less reluctantly given. The boys' delight knew no bounds, and it was a hilarious group that made things hum on the Overland Limited, as it climbed the Rockies and dropped down the western slope to the ocean. The world smiled upon them. Life ran riot within them. They had no inkling of how closely death would graze them before they even set foot upon their ship. Nor did they dream of the perils that awaited them, in days not far distant when that ship, passing through the Golden Gate, should turn its prow toward the East and breast the billows of the Pacific.

CHAPTER II

AN UNEXPECTED MEETING

The "Fearless" was a smart, staunch ship of about three thousand tons — one of a numerous fleet owned by the line of which Mr. Quinby was the manager. She had been built with special reference to the China trade, and was designed chiefly for cargoes, although she had accommodations for a considerable number of passengers. She was equipped with the latest type of modern screw engines, and although she did not run on a fixed schedule, could be counted on, almost as certainly as a regular liner, to make her port at the time appointed. Everything about the steamer was seamanlike and shipshape, and the boys were most favorably impressed, as, under the guidance of Captain Manning, they made their way forward. Here they were introduced to the first and second officers, and then shown to the quarters they were to occupy during the voyage.

Like everything else about the ship, these were trim and comfortable, and the boys were delighted to find that they had been assigned adjoiningrooms. By the time they had washed and changed their clothes, it was time for supper, and to this they did ample justice. They were valiant trenchermen, and even the narrow escape of the afternoon had not robbed them of their appetites.

"You'd better eat while you can, fellows," laughed Bert. "We sail to-morrow, and twenty-four hours from now, you may be thinking so little of food that you'll be giving it all to the fishes."

"Don't you worry," retorted Dick, "I've trolled for bluefish off the Long Island coast in half a gale, and never been seasick yet."

"Yes," said Bert, "but scudding along in a catboat is a different thing from rising and falling on the long ocean swells. We haven't any swinging cabins here to keep things always level, and the ship isn't long enough to cut through three waves at once like the big Atlantic liners."

"Well," said Tom, "if we do have to pay tribute to Neptune, I hope we won't be so badly off as the poor fellow who, the first hour, was afraid he was going to die, and, the second hour, was afraid he couldn't die."

"Don't fret about dying, boys," put in the ship's doctor, a jolly little man, with a paunch that denoted a love of good living; "You fellows are so lucky that they couldn't kill you with an axe. Though that knife did come pretty near doing the trick, didn't it? 'The sweet little cherub that sits up aloft, looking after the life of poor Jack,' was certainly working overtime, when that Malay went for you to-day."

"Yes," returned Dick, "but he slipped a cog in not looking after the poor fellow that brute wounded first. By the way, doctor, how is he? Will he live?"

"O, he'll pull through all right," answered the doctor. "I gave his wound the first rough dressing before the ambulance took him away. Luckily, the blade missed any of the vital organs, and a couple of months in the hospital will bring him around all right. That is, unless the knife was poisoned. These beggars sometimes do this, in order to make assurance doubly sure. I picked up the knife as it lay on the pier, and will turn it over to the authorities to-morrow. They'll have to use it in evidence, when the case comes up for trial."

He reached into his breast pocket as he spoke and brought out the murderous weapon. The boys shuddered as they looked at it and realized how near they had come to being its victims. They handled it gingerly as they passed it around, being very careful to avoid even a scratch, in view of what the doctor had said about the possibility of it being poisoned.

It was nearly a foot in length, with a massive handle that gave it a secure grip as well as additional force behind the stroke. The hilt was engraved with curious characters, probably an invocation to one of the malignant gods to whom it was consecrated. The blade was broad, with the edge of a razor and the point of a needle. But what gave it a peculiarly deadly and sinister significance was the wavy, crooked lines followed by the steel, and which indicated the hideous wounds it was capable of inflicting.

"Nice little toy, isn't it?" asked the doctor.

"It certainly is," replied Bert. "A bowie knife is innocent, compared with this."

"What on earth is it," asked Dick, "that makes these fellows so crazy to kill those that have never done them an injury and that they have never even seen? I can understand how the desire for revenge may prompt a man to go to such lengths to get even with an enemy, but why they attack every one without distinction is beyond me."

"Well," replied the doctor, "it's something with which reason has nothing to do. The Malays are a bloodthirsty, merciless race. They brood and sulk, until, like that old Roman emperor—Caligula, wasn't it?—they wish that the human race had only one neck, so that they could sever it with a single blow. They are sick of life and determine to end it all, but before they go, all the pent up poison of hate that has been fermenting in them finds expression in the desire to take as many as possible with them. Then too, there may be some obscure religious idea underneath it all, of offering to the gods as many victims as possible, and thus winning favor for themselves. Or, like the savage despots of Africa, who decree that when they are buried hundreds of their subjects shall be slaughtered and buried in the same grave, they may feel that their victims will have to serve them in the future world. Scientists have never analyzed the matter satisfactorily."

"Well," said Dick, as they rose from the table, "one doesn't have to be a scientist to know this much at least—that wherever a crazy Malay happens to be, it's a mighty healthy thing to be somewhere else."

"I guess nobody aboard this steamer would be inclined to dispute that," laughed the doctor, as they separated and went on deck.

Although his duties did not begin until the following day, Bert was eager beyond anything else to inspect the wireless equipment of the ship, and went at once to the wireless room, followed by the others.

It was with immense satisfaction that he established that here he had under his hand the very latest in wireless telegraphy. From the spark key to the antennae, waving from the highest mast of the ship, everything was of the most approved and up to date type. No matter how skilful the workman, he is crippled by lack of proper tools; and Bert's heart exulted as he realized that, in this respect, at least he had no reason for complaint.

"It's a dandy plant, fellows," he gloated. "There aren't many Atlantic liners have anything on this."

"How far can she talk, Bert?" asked Dick, examining the apparatus with the keenest interest.

"That depends on the weather, very largely," answered Bert. "Under almost any conditions she's good for five hundred miles, and when things are just right, two or three times as far."

"What's the limit, anyway, Bert?" asked Tom. "How far have they been able to send under the very best conditions?"

"I don't believe there is any real limit," answered Bert. "I haven't any doubt that, before many years, they'll be able to talk half way round the world. Puck, you know, in the 'Midsummer Night's Dream' boasted that he would 'put a girdle round the earth in forty minutes.' Well, the wireless will go him one better, and go round in less than forty seconds. Why, only the other day at Washington, when the weather conditions were just right, the officials there heard two stations talking to each other, off the coast of Chili, six or seven thousand miles away. Of course, ships will never talk at that distance, because they can't get a high enough mast or tower to overcome the curvature of the earth. But from land stations it is only a question of getting a high enough tower. They can talk easily now from Berlin to Sayville, Long Island, four thousand miles, by means of towers seven or eight hundred feet high. The Eiffel Tower at Paris, because still higher, has a longer range. It isn't so very long ago that they were glad enough to talk across a little creek or canal, a few feet wide. Then they tried an island, three or four miles away, then another, fourteen miles from the mainland. By the time they had done that, they knew that they had the right principle, and that it was only a matter of time before they'd bind the ends of the earth together. It started as a creeping infant; now, it's a giant, going round the world in its seven league boots."

"Hear hear," cried Dick, "how eloquent Bert is getting. He'll be dropping into poetry next."

"Well," chipped in Tom, "there is poetry sure enough in the crash of the spark and its leap out into the dark over the tumbling waves from one continent to another, but, to me, it's more like witchcraft. It's lucky Marconi didn't live two or three hundred years ago. He'd surely have been burned at the stake, for dabbling in black magic."

"Yes," rejoined Bert, "and Edison and Tesla would have kept him company. But now clear out, you fellows, and let me play with this toy of mine. I want to get next to all its quips and quirks and cranks and curves, and I can't do it with you dubs talking of poets and witches. Skip, now," and he laughingly shooed them on deck.

Left to himself, he went carefully over every detail of the equipment. Everything — detector, transmitter, tuning coil and all the other parts — were subjected to the most minute and critical inspection, and all stood the test royally. It was evident that no niggardly consideration of expense had prevented the installation of the latest and best materials. Bert's touch was almost caressing, as he handled the various parts, and his heart thrilled with a certain sense of ownership. There had been a wireless plant at one of the college buildings, and he had become very expert in its use; but hundreds of others had used it, too, and he was only one among many. Moreover, that plant had filled no part in the great world of commerce or of life, except for purposes of instruction. But this was the real thing, and from the time the steamer left the wharf until, on its return, it again swung into moorings, he would be in complete control. How many times along the invisible current would he feel the pulsing of the world's heart; what messages of joy or pain or peril would go from him or come to him, as he sat with his finger on the key and the receiver at his ear! He stood on the threshold of a new world, and it was a long time before he tore himself away, and went to rejoin his friends on the upper deck.

A young man, whose figure had something familiar about it was pacing to and fro. Bert cudgeled his memory. Of whom did it remind him? The young man turned and their eyes met. There was a start of recognition.

"Why, this must be Bert Wilson," said the newcomer, extending his hand.

"Yes," replied Bert, grasping it warmly, "and you are Ralph Quinby or his double."

"Quinby, sure enough," laughed Ralph, "and delighted to see you again. But what on earth brings you here, three thousand miles from home?"

"I expect to be twelve thousand miles from home before I get through," answered Bert; and then he told him of his engagement as wireless operator for the voyage.

"That's splendid," said Ralph, heartily. "We'll have no end of fun. I was just feeling a bit down in the mouth, because I didn't know a soul on board except the captain. You see, my father is manager of the line, and he wanted me to take the trip, so that I could enlarge my experience and be fit to step into his shoes when he gets ready to retire. So that, in a way, it's a pleasure and business trip combined."

"Here are some other fellows you know," remarked Bert, as he beckoned to Tom and Dick who came over from the rail.

They needed no introduction. A flood of memories swept over them as they shook hands. They saw again the automobile race, when Ralph in the "Gray Ghost" and Bert at the wheel of the "Red Scout" had struggled for the mastery. Before their eyes rose the crowded stands; they heard the deafening cheers and the roar of the exhausts; they saw again that last desperate spurt, when, with the throttle wide open, the "Red Scout" had challenged its gallant enemy in the stretch and flashed over the line, a winner.

That Ralph remembered it too was evident from the merry twinkle in his eyes, as he looked from one to the other of the group.

"You made me take your dust that day, all right," he said, "but I've never felt sore over that for a minute. It was a fair and square race, and the best car and the best driver won."

"Not on your life," interjected Bert, warmly. "The best car, perhaps, but not the best driver. You got every ounce of speed out of your machine that anyone could, and after all it was only a matter of inches at the finish."

"Well, it was dandy sport, anyway, win or lose," returned Ralph. "By the way, I have the 'Gray Ghost' with me now. It's crated up on the forward deck, and will be put down in the hold to-morrow. So come along now, and take a look at it."

There, sure enough, was the long, powerful, gray car, looking "fit to run for a man's life," as Ralph declared, while he patted it affectionately.

"I thought I'd bring it along," he said, "to use while we are in port at our various stopping places. It will take a good many days to unload, and then ship our return cargo, and, if the roads are good, we'll show the natives some new wrinkles in the way of fancy driving. We're all of us auto fiends, and I want you to feel that the car is as much yours as mine, all through the trip. That is," he added, mischievously, "if you fellows don't feel too haughty to ride in a car that you've already beaten."

With jest and laughter, the time passed rapidly. The evening deepened, and a hush fell over the waters of the bay. Lanterns twinkled here and there like fireflies among the shipping, while from an occasional boat rose the tinkling of a banjo or guitar. From the shore side came the night sounds of the great city, sitting proudly on her many hills and crowned with innumerable lights. Silence gathered over the little group, as they gazed, and each was busy with his own thoughts. This loved land of theirs—by this time to-morrow, it would be out of sight below the horizon. Who knew when they would see it again, or through what perils they might pass before they once more touched its shores? It was the little shiver before the plunge, as they stood upon the brink of the unknown; and they were a trifle more quiet than usual, when at last they said good-night and sought forgetfulness in sleep.

CHAPTER III

A STARTLING MESSAGE

The next morning, all was stir and bustle on board the steamer. The great cranes groaned, as they hoisted aboard the last of the freight, and lowered it into the hold, that gaped like a huge monster, whose appetite could never be satiated. Men were running here and there, in obedience to the hoarse commands of the mates, and bringing order out of the apparent confusion. The pier and decks were thronged with friends and relatives of the passengers, come to say good-by to those who seemed to become doubly dear, as the hour of parting drew near. The cabins were piled with flowers that, under the inexorable rules of sea-going ships, would have to be thrown overboard, as soon as the vessel had cleared the harbor. Everywhere there were tears and smiles and hand grasps, as friends looked into each other's eyes, with the unspoken thought that the parting "might be for years, or it might be forever."

The boys had risen early, and, after a hearty breakfast, had come on deck, where they watched with keenest zest the preparations for the start. It was a glorious day and one that justified all they had heard of the wonderful California climate. The sun was bright, but not oppressive, and a delightful breeze blew up from the bay. The tang of the sea was in their nostrils, and, as they gazed over the splendid panorama spread out before them, their spirits rose and their hearts swelled with the mere joy of living. The slight melancholy of the night before had vanished utterly, and something of the old Viking spirit stirred within them, as they sniffed the salt breeze and looked toward the far horizon where the sky and waves came together. They, too, were Argonauts, and who knew what Golden Fleece of delight and adventure awaited their coming, in the enchanting empires of the East, or in the

"Summer isles of Eden, lyingIn dark purple spheres of sea."

As they stood at the rail, filling their lungs with the invigorating air, and watching the animated scenes about them, Ralph came up to them, accompanied by an alert, keen-eyed man, whom he introduced as his father.

He shook hands cordially with the boys, but when he learned that Dick and Tom, as well as Bert, were all students in the college from which he had himself graduated, his cordiality became enthusiasm. He was one of the men who, despite the passing of the years and the growth of business cares, remain young in heart, and he was soon laughing and chatting as gaily as the boys themselves. There was nothing of the snob about him, despite his wealth and prominence, and, in this respect Ralph was "a chip of the old block."

"So you are the Wilson whose fadeaway ball won the pennant, are you?" as he turned to Bert. "By George, I'd like to have seen that last game. The afternoon that game was played, I had the returns sent in over a special wire in my office. And when you forged ahead and then held down their heavy hitters in the ninth, I was so excited that I couldn't keep still, but just got up and paced the floor, until I guess my office force thought I was going crazy. But you turned the trick, all right, and saved my tottering reason," he added, jovially.

The boys laughed. "It's lucky I didn't know all that," grinned Bert, "or I might have got so nervous that they would have knocked me out of the box. But since you are so interested, let me show you a memento of the game." And running below, he was back in a minute with the souvenir presented to him by the college enthusiasts.

It was a splendid gift. The identical ball with which he had struck out the opposing team's most dangerous slugger in the ninth had been encased in a larger ball of solid gold on which Bert's name had been engraved, together with the date and score of the famous game. Now it was passed from hand to hand amid loud expressions of admiration.

"It's certainly a beauty," commented Mr. Quinby, "and my only regret is that I wasn't called upon to contribute toward getting it. I suppose it will be rather hard on you fellows," he went on, "to have to go without any baseball this summer. If I know you rightly, you'd rather play than eat."

"Oh, well," broke in Ralph, "they may be able to take a fling at it once in a while, even if they are abroad. It used to be the 'national' game, but it is getting so popular everywhere that we'll soon have to call it the 'international' game. In Japan, especially, there are some corking good teams, and they play the game for all it is worth. Take the nine of Waseda University, and they'd give Yale or Princeton all they wanted to do to beat them. Last year, they hired a big league star to come all the way from America, to act as coach. They don't have enough 'beef,' as a rule, to make them heavy sluggers, but they are all there in bunting and place hitting, and they are like cats on the bases."

"Yes," said Dick, "and, even leaving foreigners out of the question, the crews from Uncle Sam's warships have what you might call a Battleship League among themselves, and every vessel has its nine. Feeling runs high when they are in port, and the games are as hotly contested as though a World's Series were in question. I'm told that, at the time of the Boxer rebellion, there were some dandy games played by our boys right under the walls of Peking."

Just here the captain approached, and, with a hearty handshake and best wishes for the journey, Mr. Quinby went forward with him to discuss business details connected with the trip.

Ten o'clock, the hour set for starting, was at hand. The first bell, warning all visitors ashore, had already rung. The last bale of freight had been lowered into the hold and the hatches battened down. There was the usual rush of eleventh hour travelers, as the taxis and cabs rattled down to the piers and discharged their occupants. All the passengers were on the shore side of the vessel, calling to their friends on the dock, the women waving their handkerchiefs, at one moment, and, the next, putting them to their eyes. The last bell rang, the huge gangplank swung inward, there was a tinkling signal in the engine room and the propellers began slowly to revolve. The steamer turned down the bay, passed the Golden Gate where the sea lions sported around the rocks, and out into the mighty Pacific. The voyage of the Fearless had begun.

Down in the wireless room, Bert had buckled to his work. With the telephone receiver held close to his ears by a band passing over his head, he exchanged messages with the land they were so rapidly leaving behind them, with every revolution of the screws. Amid the crashing of the sounder and the spitting blue flames, he felt perfectly in his element. Here was work, here was usefulness, here was power, here was life. Between this stately vessel, with its costly cargo and still more precious freight of human lives, and the American continent, he was the sole connecting link. Through him alone, father talked with son, husband with wife, captain with owner, friend with friend. Without him, the vessel was a hermit, shut out from the world at large; with him, it still held its place in the universal life.

But this undercurrent of reflection and exultation did not, for a moment, distract him from his work. The messages came in rapidly. He knew they would. The first day at sea is always the busiest one. There were so many last injunctions, so many things forgotten in the haste of farewell, that he was taxed to the utmost to keep his work well in hand. Fortunately he was ambidextrous, could use his left hand almost as readily as his right, and this helped him immensely. From an early age, more from fun than anything else, he had cultivated writing with either hand, without any idea that the day would come when this would prove a valuable practical accomplishment. Now with one finger on the key, he rapidly wrote down the messages with the other, and thus was able to double the rapidity and effectiveness of his work.

Before long there was a lull in the flood of messages, and when time came for dinner, he signaled the San Francisco office to hold up any further communications for an hour or so, threw off his receiver, and joined his friends at the table.

"Well, Bert, how does she go?" asked Dick, who sat at his right, while Tom and Ralph faced them across the table.

"Fine," answered Bert, enthusiastically. "It isn't work; it's pleasure. I'm so interested in it that I almost grudge the time it takes to eat, and that's something new for me."

"It must be getting serious, if it hits you as hard as that," said Tom, in mock concern. "I'll have to give the doctor a tip to keep his eye on you."

"Oh, Bert just says that, so that when he gets seasick, he'll have a good excuse for not coming to meals," chaffed Ralph.

"Well, watch me, fellows, if you think my appetite is off," retorted Bert, as he attacked his food with the avidity of a wolf.

"By the way," asked Dick, "what arrangements have you made for any message that may come, while you are toying with your dinner in this languid fashion?"

"I've told the San Francisco man to hold things up for a while," replied Bert. "That's the only station we're likely to hear from just now, and the worst of the rush is over. After we get out of range of the land stations, all that we'll get will be from passing ships, and that will only be once in a while."

"Of course," he went on, "theoretically, there ought to be someone there every minute of the twenty-four hours. You might be there twenty-three hours and fifty-nine minutes, and nothing happen. But, in the last minute of the twenty-fourth hour, there might be something of vital importance. You know when that awful wreck occurred last year, the operator was just about to take the receiver from his head, when he caught the call. One minute later, and he wouldn't have heard it and over eight hundred people would have been lost."

"I suppose," said Ralph, "that, as a matter of fact, there ought to be two or three shifts, so that someone could be on hand all the time. I know that the

Company is considering something of the kind, but 'large bodies move slowly,' and they haven't got to it yet."

"For my part," chimed in Tom, "I should think that with all the brains that are working on the subject, there would have been some way devised to make a record of every call, and warn the operator at any minute of the day or night."

"They're trying hard to get something practical," said Bert. "Marconi himself is testing out a plan that he thinks will work all right. His idea is to get a call that will be really one long dash, so that it won't be confounded with any letter of the alphabet. He figures on making this so strong that it will pass through a very sensitive instrument with sufficient force to ring a bell, that will be at the bedside of the operator."

"Rather rough on a fellow, don't you think?" joined in the ship's doctor. "If he were at all nervous, he might lie there awake, waiting for the bell to ring. It reminds me of a friend of mine, who once put up at a country hotel. He was told that the man who slept in the next room was very irritable and a mere bundle of nerves. He couldn't bear the least noise, and my friend promised to keep it in mind. He was out rather late that night, and when he started to retire he dropped one of his shoes heavily on the floor. Just then he remembered his nervous neighbor. He went on undressing quietly, walked about on tiptoe, put out the light, and crept into bed. Just as he was going off to sleep, a voice came from the other room: 'Say, when in thunder are you going to drop that other shoe?'"

"In the meantime," went on Bert, when the laugh had subsided, "they've got an ingenious device on some of the British ships. It seems rather cruel, because they have to use a frog. You know how sensitive frogs are to electricity. Well, they attach a frog to the receiving end, and under him they put a sheet of blackened paper. As the dots and dashes come in, the current jerks the frog's legs over the paper. The leg scrapes the black away, and leaves white dots and dashes. So that you can pick up the paper and read the message just like any other, except that the letters are white instead of black."

"Poor old frogs," said Ralph. "If they knew enough, they'd curse the very name of electricity. Galvani started with them in the early days, and they've still got to 'shake a leg' in the interest of science."

"Yes," murmured Tom, "it's simply shocking."

He ducked as Ralph made a playful pass at him.

"There's been quite a stir caused by it," went on Bert, calmly ignoring Tom's awful pun, "and the humane societies are taking it up. The probability is that it will be abolished. It certainly does seem cruel."

"I don't know," said the doctor. "Like many other questions, there are two sides to it. We all agree that no pain should be inflicted upon poor dumb animals, unless there is some great good to be gained by it. But it is a law of life that the lesser must give way to the greater. We use the cow to get vaccine for small-pox, the horse to supply the anti-toxin for diphtheria. Rabbits and mice and guinea-pigs and monkeys we inoculate with the germs of cancer and consumption, in order to study the causes of these various diseases, and, perhaps, find a remedy for them. All this seems barbarous and cruel; but the common sense of mankind agrees that it would be far more cruel to let human beings suffer and die by the thousands, when these experiments may save them. If the twitching of a frog's leg should save a vessel from shipwreck, we would have to overlook the frog's natural reluctance to write the message. I hope, though," he concluded, as he pushed back his chair, "that they'll soon find something else that will do just as well, and leave the frog in his native puddle."

When they reached the deck, they found that the breeze had freshened, and, with the wind on her starboard quarter, the Fearless was bowling along in capital style. Her engines were working powerfully and rhythmically, and everything betokened a rapid run to Hawaii, which the captainfigured on reaching in about eight days. The more seasoned travelers were wrapped in rugs and stretched out in steamer chairs, but many of the others had already sought the seclusion of their staterooms. It was evident that there would be an abundance of empty seats at the table that evening.

Throughout the rest of the day the messages were few and far between. Before that time next day, they would probably have ceased altogether as far as the land stations were concerned, and from that time on until they reached Hawaii, the chief communications would be from passing ships within the wireless range.

The boys were gathered in the wireless room that night, telling stories and cracking jokes, when suddenly Bert's ear caught a click. He straightened up and listened eagerly. Then his face went white and his eyes gleamed with excitement. It was the S. O. S. signal, the call of deadly need and peril. A moment more and he leaped to his feet.

"Call the captain, one of you fellows, quick," he cried.

For this was the message that had winged its way over the dark waste of waters:

"Our ship is on fire. Latitude 37:12, longitude 126:17. For God's sake, help."

CHAPTER IV

THE FLAMING SHIP

The captain came in hurriedly and read the message. He figured out the position.

"She's all of sixty miles away," he said, looking up from his calculation, "and even under forced draught we can't reach her in less than three hours. Tell her we're coming," he ordered, and hurried out to give the necessary directions.

The course of the ship was altered at once, the engines were signaled for full speed ahead, and with her furnaces roaring, she rushed through the night to the aid of her sister vessel, sorely beset by the most dreaded peril of the sea.

In the mean time Bert had clicked off the message: "We've got you, old man. Ship, Fearless, Captain Manning. Longitude 125:20, latitude 36:54. Will be with you in three hours. Cheer up. If you're not disabled, steam to meet us."

Quickly the answer came back: "Thank God. Fighting the fire, but it's getting beyond us. Hasn't reached the engine room yet, but may very soon. Hurry."

In short, jerky sentences came the story of the disaster. The steamer was the Caledonian, a tramp vessel, plying between Singapore and San Francisco. There was a heavy cargo and about forty passengers. A little while since, they had detected fire in the hold, but had concealed the fact from the passengers and had tried to stifle it by their own efforts. It had steadily gained, however, despite their desperate work, until the flames burst through the deck. A wild panic had ensued, but the captain and the mates had kept the upper hand. The crew had behaved well, and the boats were ready for launching if the worst came to the worst. The fire was gaining. "Hurry. Captain says— —"

Then the story ceased. Bert called and called again. No answer. The boys looked at each other.

"The dynamo must have gone out of commission," said Bert. "I can't get him. The flames may have driven him out of the wireless room."

All were in an agony of suspense and fear. It seemed as though they crept, although the ship shook with the vibration of its powerful engines, working as they had never worked before. The Fearless was fairly flying, as though she knew the fearful need of haste.

Outside of the wireless room, none of the passengers knew of the disaster. Most of them had retired, and, if the few who were still up and about sensed anything unusual, the discipline of the ship kept questions unspoken. All the officers and the crew, however, were on the alert and tingling with the strain, and every eye was turned toward the distant horizon, to catch the first glimpse of the burning vessel.

Out into the night, Bert sent his call desperately, hoping to raise some other ship nearer to the doomed steamer than the Fearless, but in vain. He caught a collier, three hundred miles away, and a United States gunboat, one hundred and sixty miles distant, but, try as he would, there was nothing nearer. Nobody but themselves could attempt the rescue. Of course, there was the chance that some sailing vessel, not equipped with wireless, might come upon the scene, but this was so remote that it could be dismissed from consideration.

More than half the distance had been covered when Dick, who had stepped outside, came running in.

"Come on out, fellows," he cried, excitedly. "We can see a light in the sky that we think must come from the fire."

They followed him on the run. There, sure enough, on the distant horizon, was a deep reddish glow, that seemed to grow brighter with every passing moment. At times, it waned a trifle, probably obscured by smoke, only to reappear more crimson than ever, as the vessel drew nearer.

"How far off do you suppose it is now?" asked Tom.

"Not more than fifteen miles, I should think," answered Bert. "We'll be there in less than an hour now, if we can keep up this pace."

The Fearless flew on, steadily cutting down the distance, and now the sky was the color of blood. Everything had been gotten in readiness for the work of rescue. The boats had been cleared and hung in their davits, ready to be lowered in a trice. Lines of hose were prepared, not so much with the hope of putting out the fire as to protect their own vessel from the flying brands. Every man of the crew was at his appointed place. Since the wireless could no longer be used to send messages of encouragement, rockets were sent up at intervals to tell the unfortunates that help was coming.

"Look!" cried Tom. "That was an actual flash I saw that time."

Gradually these became more frequent, and now the upper part of the vessel came into view, wreathed in smoke and flame. Soon the hull appeared, and then they could get a clear idea of the catastrophe.

The whole forward part of the vessel was a seething mass of fire. The engines had been put out of commission, and the hull wallowed helplessly at the mercy of the waves. The officers and crew, fighting to the last, had been crowded aft, and the stern was black with passengers huddled despairingly together. The supply of boats had been insufficient, and two of these had been smashed in lowering. Two others, packed to the guards, had been pushed away from the vessel, so as not to be set on fire by the brands that fell in showers all around. Near the stern, some of the sailors were hastily trying to improvise a raft with spars and casks. They were working with superhuman energy, but, hampered as they were by the frantic passengers, could make but little progress. And all the time the pitiless flames were coming nearer and nearer, greedily licking up everything that disputed their advance. It was a scene of anguish and of panic such as had never been dreamed of by the breathless spectators who crowded the bow of the Fearless, as it swiftly swept into the zone of light and prepared to lower its boats.

Suddenly there was a great commotion visible on the flaming ship. They had seen their rescuers. Men shouted and pointed wildly; women screamed and fell on their knees in thanksgiving. The boats already in the water gave way and made for the Fearless. The sailors stopped work upon the raft, now no longer needed, and turned to with the officers who were striving desperately to keep the more frenzied passengers from plunging headlong into the sea and swimming to the steamer. Their last refuge in the stern had grown pitifully small now, and the flames, gathering volume as they advanced, rushed toward them as though determined not to be balked of the prey that had seemed so surely in their grasp.

It was a moment for quick action, and Captain Manning rose to the occasion. In obedience to his sharp word of command, the sailors tumbled into the boats, and these were dropped so smartly that they seemed to hit the water together. Out went the oars and away they pulled with all the strength and practised skill of their sinewy arms. Bert and Dick were permitted to go as volunteers in the boat of Mr. Collins, the first mate, who had given his consent with some reluctance, as he had little faith in any but regular sailors in cases of this kind; and his boat was the first to reach the vessel and round to under the stern.

"Women and children first," the unwritten law of the sea, was strictly enforced, and they were lowered one by one, until the boat sat so low in the water that Mr. Collins ordered his crew to back away and let the next one take its place. Just as it got under way, a woman holding a baby in her arms, frantic with fright as she saw the boat leaving, broke away from the restraining hand of a sailor, and leaped from the stern. She missed the gig, which was fortunate, as she would certainly have capsized it, heavily laden as it already was, and fell into the water. In an instant Bert, who could swim like a fish, had plunged in and grabbed her as she rose to the surface. A few strokes of the oars and they were hauled aboard, and the boat made for the ship. Collins, a taciturn man, looked his approval but said nothing at the time, although, in a talk with the captain afterwards, he went so far as to revise his opinion of volunteers and to admit that an able seaman could have done no better.

The rest of the passengers were quickly taken off and then came the turn of the officers and crew. The captain was the last to leave the devoted vessel, and it was with a warm grasp of sympathy and understanding that Captain Manning greeted him as he came over the side. He was worn with the strain and shaken with emotion. He had done all that a man could do to save his ship, but fate had been too strong for him and he had to bow to the inevitable. He refused to go below and take some refreshment, but stood with knitted brows and folded arms watching the burning steamer that had carried his hopes and fortunes. They respected his grief and left him alone for a time, while they made arrangements for the homeless passengers and crew.

These were forlorn enough. They had saved practically no baggage and only the most cherished of their personal belongings. Some had been badly burned in their efforts to subdue the flames, and all were at the breaking point from excitement and fatigue. The doctors of both ships were taxed to the utmost, administering sedatives and tonics and dressing the wounds of the injured. By this time the passengers of the Fearless had, of course, been roused by the tumult, and men and women alike vied with each other in aiding the unfortunates. Cabins and staterooms were prepared for the passengers, while quarters in the forecastle were provided for the crew who, with the proverbial stolidity and fatalism of their kind, soon made themselves at home, taking the whole thing as a matter of course. They had just been at hand-grips with death; but this had occurred to them so often that they regarded it simply as an incident of their calling.

There was no thought of sleep for Bert that night. The sounder crashed and the blue flames leaped for hours in the wireless room. The operator of the Caledonian volunteered to help him, but Bert wouldn't hear of it and sent him to his bunk, where, after the terrific strain, he was soon in the sleep of utter exhaustion.

Then Bert called up the San Francisco station and told his story. The owners of the ship were notified that the vessel and cargo were a total loss, but that all the passengers had been saved. They sent their thanks to Captain Manning and then wirelessed for details. Mr. Quinby, of course, was called into the conference. Now that it was settled that no lives had been lost, the most important question was as to the disposition of passengers and crew. They had been making for San Francisco, but naturally it was out of the question for the Fearless to relinquish her voyage and take them into port.

Three courses were open. They could go to Hawaii, the first stopping place, and there take the first steamer leaving for San Francisco. Or they could depend on the chance of meeting some vessel homeward bound, to which they could transship before reaching Honolulu. Or Bert could send his call abroad through his wireless zone and perhaps arrange for some ship coming toward them to sail along a certain course, meet them at a given location and there take charge of the Caledonian's people. In that case, the owners, of course, would expect to recompense them handsomely for their time and trouble.

As the survivors were desperately anxious to reach home and friends at the earliest possible moment, Bert was instructed to follow the latter course and do his utmost to raise some approaching vessel. For a long time his efforts were fruitless. His call flew over the ocean wastes but awoke no answering echo. At last, however, well toward morning, his eager ear caught a responsive click. It came from the Nippon, one of the trans-Pacific liners plying between Yokohama and San Francisco. She was less than four hundred miles away and coming on a line slightly east of the Fearless. The situation was explained, and after the captains of the two steamers had carried on a long conversation, it was agreed that the Nippon should take charge of the survivors. They would probably meet late that afternoon, and arrangements were made to keep each other informed hourly of pace and direction, until they should come in sight.

Bert breathed a huge sigh of relief when that question was settled. But his work was not yet done. He must notify the United States Government of the presence of the derelict as a menace to navigation. The Caledonian had lost all its upper works and part of the hull had been consumed. But the waves breaking over it as it lurched from side to side had kept it from burning to the water's edge, and it now tossed about, a helpless hulk right in the lane of ships. So many vessels have been lost by coming in collision with such floating wrecks at night, that the Government maintains a special line of gunboats, whose one duty is to search them out and blow them up with dynamite. Bert gave the exact latitude and longitude to the San Francisco operator, who promised to forward it at once to the Navy Department at Washington.

Then, at last, Bert leaned back in his chair and relaxed. The strain upon heart and nerve and brain had been tremendous. But he had "stood the gaff." The first great test had been nobly met. Cool, clever, self-reliant, he had not flinched or wavered under the load of responsibility. The emergency had challenged him and he had mastered it. In this work, so new to him, he had kept his courage and borne himself as a veteran of the key.

He patted the key affectionately. Good old wireless! How many parts it had played that night and how well! Telling first of pain and terror and begging for help; then cheerily sending hope and comfort and promise of salvation. Without it, the dawn would now be breaking on two small boats and a flimsy raft, crowded with miserable refugees and tossing up and down on the gray waves that threatened to engulf. Now they were safe, thank God, warm and snug and secure, soon to be called to the abundant breakfast, whose savory odors already assailed his nostrils. And now the whole world knew of the disaster and the rescue; and the machinery of the Government was moving with reference to that abandoned hulk; and a great ship was bounding toward them over the trackless waste to meet at a given place and time and take the survivors back to country and home and friends and love and life. It was wonderful, mysterious, unbelievable— —

A touch upon his shoulder roused him from his reverie, and he looked up, to see the captain standing beside him.

"You've done great work this night, Wilson," he said, smiling gravely, "and I'll see that the owners hear of it. But now you must be dead tired, and I want you to get your breakfast and turn in for a while. I'll get Howland, the wireless man of the Caledonian, to hold things down for a few hours, while you get a rest. I've told the cook to get a bite ready for you and then I want you to tumble in."

The "bite" resolved itself into a capacious meal of steak and eggs, reinforced by fragrant coffee, after which, obeying orders, he rolled into his bunk and at once fell into deep and dreamless sleep.

Meanwhile, the ship awoke to the life of a new day. The sun streamed down from cloudless skies and a spanking breeze blew over the quarter. The air was like wine and to breathe it was an inspiration. The sea smiled and dimpled as its myriad waves reflected back the glorious light. TheFearless slipped through the long swells as swiftly as a water sprite, "footing it featly" on her road to Hawaii, the Paradise of the Pacific. Everything spoke of life and buoyancy, and the terrible events of the night before might well have been a frightful nightmare from which they had happily awakened.

There were grim reminders, however, that it had been more than a dream in the hurrying doctors, the bandaged hands and faces, the haggard features of the men and the semi-hysterical condition of some of the women. But there had been no death or mortal injury. The Red Death had gazed upon them with its flaming eyes and scorched them with its baleful breath, but they had not been consumed. There were property losses, but no wife had been snatched from her husband, no mother wailed for her child. Under the comforting influence of a hot breakfast, the heartfelt sympathy of the passengers and the invigorating air and sunshine, they gradually grew more cheerful. After all, they were alive, snatched by a miracle from a hideous death; and how could or dared they complain of minor ills? The tension relaxed as the hours wore on, and by the time that Bert, after a most refreshing sleep, appeared again on deck the scene was one of animation and almost gaiety.

Straight to the wireless room he went, to be met on the threshold by Dick and Tom and Ralph, who gathered around him in tumultuous greeting.

"Bully for you, old man," cried Dick. "We hear that you did yourself proud last night."

"Yes," chimed in Ralph. "I wouldn't dare to tell you what Father says in a message I've just received, or you'd have a swelled head, sure."

"Nonsense," answered Bert. "I simply did what it was up to me to do. Good morning, Mr. Howland," he said, as the young fellow seated at the key rose to greet him. "How are things going?"

"Just jogging along," answered Howland. "I guess you cleaned up about everything before you turned in. We're getting beyond the shore range, but I've been keeping in touch every hour with the Nippon. The captain figures that we'll get together at about four this afternoon."

The former operator of the Caledonian was a well set-up, clear-eyed young fellow, about the age of Bert and his chums, and a liking sprang up between them at once. With the recuperative power of youth he had almost entirely recovered from the events of the night before, although his singed hair and eyebrows bore eloquent testimony to the perils he had faced and so narrowly escaped. He had stuck to his post until the blistering heat had made life impossible in the wireless room, and then had done yeoman's work in aiding the officers and crew to fight the fire and maintain order among the passengers. The boys listened with keenest interest, while he went over in graphic style his personal experiences.

"I can't tell you how I felt when I got your message," he said, as he turned to Bert. "I had about given up hope when your answer came. I rushed at once to the captain and he passed the word to the passengers and crew. It put new heart and life into them all, and it was the only thing that kept many from jumping into the sea when the flames got so horribly near. But they held on desperately, and when they saw your rockets I wish you could have heard the cry that went up. They knew then that it was only a matter of minutes before your boats would be under the stern. But it was fearfully close figuring," he went on, soberly. "You saw yourself that fifteen minutes after the last boat pulled away the whole stern was a mass of flames."

"Well," said Bert, as he slipped on the receiver, and took charge of the key, "it's lucky that I got your call just when I did. A little later and I'd have been off duty."

"That reminds me," broke in Ralph. "I sent a message to Father to-day about that, urging that you have an assistant to take charge when you are at meals or in bed. I suggested, too, that since Mr. Howland was here, he might be willing to go on with us and act as your assistant. He says he is agreeable if they want him to, and I expect a wireless from Father to the captain authorizing him to make the arrangement."

"I hope he will," said Bert, warmly. "Accidents have an awkward way of happening just when they ought not to, and when one thinks of the life and property at stake it certainly seems that somebody should be on the job all the time."

A little later the looked-for message came instructing Captain Manning to engage Howland as Bert's deputy during the voyage. From now on, there would not be one moment of the twenty-four hours that someone would not be on watch to send or receive, much to Bert's relief and delight. Now he could breathe freely and enjoy his work, without any torturing fears of what might have happened while he slept.

By half-past three that afternoon the ships were within twenty miles of each other. The beautiful weather still continued and the sea was as "calm as a millpond." All were on the alert to greet the oncoming steamer. Soon a dot appeared, growing rapidly larger until it resolved itself into a magnificent steamer, seven hundred feet in length, with towering masts and deck piled on deck, crowded with dense masses of people. She made a stately picture as she came on until a quarter of a mile from the Fearless. Then she hove to and lowered her boats.

With deep emotion and the warmest thanks, the survivors bade their rescuers good-by and were carried over to the Nippon, their third temporary home within twenty-four hours. By the time the last boat had unloaded and been swung on board, dusk had fallen. The ships squared away on their separate courses and the bells in the engine room signaled full speed ahead. Handkerchiefs waved and whistles tooted as they passed each other, and the white-coated band on the upper deck of the Nippon played "Home Again." The electric lights were suddenly turned on and the great ship glowed in beauty from stem to stern. They watched her as she drew swiftly away, until her gleaming lights became tiny diamonds on the horizon's rim and then faded into the night.

CHAPTER V

AN ISLAND PARADISE

"Land ho!" shouted the look-out from his airy perch in the crow's nest, and with one accord the passengers of the Fearless rushed on deck to catch the first glimpse of that wonderful land they had all heard so much about. Hawaii! What a vision of hill and plain, of mountain and valley, of dangerous precipice and treacherous canyon, of sandy beach and waving palm, of radiant sunshine and brilliant moonlight, the magic of that name evokes!

"Gee, fellows, can you see anything that looks like land?" Bert asked of his companions, as they elbowed their way through the crowd to the railing of the ship. "Oh, yes, there it is," he cried a moment later, pointing to a tiny spot on the horizon, "but it looks as if it were hundreds of miles away."

"It sure does," Dick agreed. "If this atmosphere were not so remarkably clear, we wouldn't be able to see it at all. It doesn't matter how far away it is, though, as long as it's in sight. For the last few days it has seemed to me that we would never reach it," and he gazed longingly at the speck on the horizon that seemed to be dissolving into two or three smaller parts that became more distinct every moment.

"Yes, I can't wait to try the little old 'Gray Ghost' on some of those swell Hawaiian roads. Say, fellows, can't you just imagine yourselves in the old car; can't you feel the throb of the motor and the whistling of the wind in your ears as she takes a steep hill with a 'give me something hard, won't you' air? Can't you?" he demanded, joyfully, while the boys thrilled at the mere prospect.

"You bet your life," Tom agreed, enthusiastically. "Make believe we won't make things hum in little old Hawaii, eh, fellows?" and they all laughed from sheer delight.

"Glad to find you in such good spirits this fine morning, boys," came a genial voice behind them and the boys turned to find the doctor regarding them with a good-natured smile on his friendly face. "I don't wonder you feel good at the prospect of setting foot on solid ground again. For, no matter how enjoyable and prosperous the voyage may be, one is always glad to get on shore and feel that he may come and go when he pleases and is not at the mercy of the elements. I for one will be glad when we cast anchor."

"I have always heard that Hawaii was one of the most beautiful countries in the world, and I've always wanted to see it," said Bert. "What do you think of it, Doctor? You must have been here many times."

Dr. Hamilton took two or three long puffs of his cigar before he answered, reflectively, "It has always seemed to me that when Nature discovered Hawaii she had some time on her hands that she didn't know what to do with, so she spent it in making this obscure little group of islands way out in the Pacific, the garden spot of the world. Over those islands the wind never blows too roughly or too coldly, the sun never shines too brightly and there is no snow to blight and kill the vegetation that warm rain and summer sun have called forth. Over there the grass is greener, the sky bluer and the scenery more beautiful than it is in any other part of the world. If you should take everything that you consider beautiful, multiply it by one hundred and put them in one small portion of the earth, you would have some idea of what Hawaii is like."

The boys were struck by the outburst.

"Hawaii is the doctor's favorite hobby," Ralph said, in response to the look of astonishment and wonder on the boys' faces. "If he had his way, he'd live here all the year round."

"That I would," said the doctor, with a sigh, "but my profession claims me first, last and all the time. However," he added, with his cheerful smile, "I want you boys to make the most of the few days we are to spend here, to have the time of your lives. The only thing I ask of you is that you don't run the 'Gray Ghost' over the side of a precipice or seek to inquire too closely into the mysteries of the firepit, Halemaumau. I'll have to leave you, as I have some important matters to attend to before I can enjoy the beauties of Hawaii. Coming, Bert? Yes, I shouldn't wonder if we would be getting some wireless messages very soon."

The three companions watched Bert and the doctor until they disappeared down the companion-way and then turned once more to the islands.

After a moment of silence Tom said, "Say, if Hawaii is all the doctor says it is, Ralph, we ought to have some fun. Imagine driving the machine along a precipice and visiting fire-pits with outlandish names. What was it he called it?"

"Halemaumau," Ralph answered. "It is a jaw-breaker, isn't it, but I've heard Dad talk so much about Hawaiian wonders that I've got the name down pat. You see Halemaumau means 'House of Everlasting Fire,' and it's the name of the fire-pit of the crater, Kilauea. There, don't you think I've mastered the subject and learned my lesson well?"

"You have, indeed, my son," Dick said, assuming his best grandfatherly air. "If you continue on the road you have begun you will make a success of your life."

"Say, fellows," Tom broke in. "Stop your nonsense and look at what you're coming to. I'm beginning to think that Dr. Hamilton didn't exaggerate, after all. Just look at that line of beach with the cliffs behind it, forming a dark background for the white of the buildings. And what are those funny, bobbing things in the water? I suppose they must be boats of some sort, but they don't look like anything I ever saw."

"I guess they must be the boats of the native money divers."

"Money divers!" Tom exclaimed. "Where do they get the money?"

"We give it to them," said Dick. "I remember reading about how passengers throw their perfectly good money into the water just for the fun of seeing those little grafters pick it up. A waste of good money I call it."

"Gee, I'm going into the business," Tom affirmed. "Just give me a diving costume and I bet you couldn't tell me from the natives."

"You needn't count on annexing any of my hard-earned cash, because you won't get it. I'd be more likely to throw a dynamite bomb in just as you were getting ready to dive," Dick said.

"I know you would, you old skinflint. The only thing is that you would be just as likely as I to get blown up. I guess you left that out of your calculations, didn't you?"

"What's all this about dynamite bombs and getting blown up?" Bert asked, coming up behind them. "It sounds rather bloodthirsty."

"Oh, he's just threatening my very valuable life," Tom answered, "but I forgive him, for he's not responsible for what he says. To change the subject, what are you doing up here when you ought to be taking down wireless messages?"

"Oh, I'm off duty for a few days, now. I'm glad of it, for, although I like nothing better than taking down messages and sending them out, it's good to have a few days to explore this country that the doctor has recommended so highly. It sure does look promising."

By this time the Fearless had weighed anchor and the boats were being let down to convey the passengers to the shore. All around the ship were the queer little craft of the natives, the occupants on the alert to catch the first bit of money thrown to them. They had not long to wait, for soon small pieces of coin were being showered down. As each piece fell into the water, the little brown-skinned native boys would dive in after it and catch it, with a deftness born of long experience, before it reached the bottom. In spite of the boys' declared intentions not to waste their "hard-earned and carefully-hoarded cash," a few pieces of that very same cash went to increase the spoils of one especially active and dextrous young native. No matter how hard they tried to be prudent or how emphatically they declared that "this would surely be the last bit of money that that little rascal would get out of them," another coin would find its way into the eager hands of the little dark-skinned tempter. There was a very strong bond of fellowship between this small native diving for money way off in the islands of the Pacific and the strong, sturdy college boys who had fought so gallantly on the diamond for the glory of Alma Mater. It was the call of the expert to the expert, the admiration of one who has "done things" for the accomplishments of another.

However, the boys were not very sorry when they reached the shore where they were beyond temptation. Tom voiced the general sentiment when he said, "Gee, if we hadn't touched land just as we did, I'd have had to telegraph home to Dad for more money. They nearly broke me."

While they were waiting for Ralph, who had stayed behind to see that the "Gray Ghost" got over safely on the raft rigged up for the purpose, the comrades took a look around them. And there was enough to occupy their attention for an hour just in the country in the immediate neighborhood of the harbor. All around them swarmed the natives, big, powerful, good-natured people, all with a smile of welcome on their dark faces. Everywhere was bustle and life and activity.

"I always thought that Hawaii was a slow sort of place," Dick said, "but it seems that I was mistaken. This crowd rivals the business crush on Fifth Avenue."

"It does that," said Bert. "But just take a glance at this scenery, my friends. Did you ever see anything on Fifth Avenue that looked like that?"

"Well, hardly. But it's the town that takes my eye. Look at those quaint houses and the big white building—I suppose it must be a hotel—towering over them. And isn't that a picture, that avenue with the double border of palm trees? We must explore that first thing when we get the 'Gray Ghost.' Say, I'm glad I came."

"So am I," said Tom. "If it hadn't been for you, Bert, we shouldn't any of us be here. Prof. Gilbert didn't know what a public benefactor he was when he nominated you for the telegraphy job. Say, isn't that the car coming over now?" he asked, pointing to a great raft that was heading slowly for the dock.

"It looks like it," Bert replied. "Make believe it won't seem good to be in a car again. I'm anxious to get my belongings up to one of the hotels, too."

"Yes, I'm glad we decided to stay in a hotel for the few days we are going to spend here. It will be good to be able to eat our breakfast on shore for a little while instead of on the briny deep," said Tom, who had not been altogether free from occasional pangs of sea-sickness during the voyage.

By this time the raft had landed the car and the other luggage. Ralph was beside his favorite, looking it over from one end to the other to see that everything was intact, while a crowd of curious little urchins watched his every action. In a moment our three fellows had joined him and were busily engaged in trying to remedy an imaginary fault. They finally gave this up as a hopeless task as the car was in absolutely perfect condition.

"I guess there's nothing very much the matter with the old car, eh, fellows?" said Ralph with the pride of possession in his voice. "I shouldn't wonder if she could show the natives something of the art of racing and hill-climbing. I bet she is just as anxious as we are to try her speed on that palm avenue there."

"Don't let's waste any time then," Dick suggested. "What's the matter with piling our luggage into the car and going right over to the hotel? By the way," he added, as a second thought, "what hotel are we going to?"

"Why, Dad told me that if we wanted to get off the ship at Hawaii that the best place to put up at would be the Seaside House," said Ralph. "He thinks that we can have more fun at a small place than we could at one of the swell hotels."

"I agree with him there," said Bert, "but do you know the way?"

"You just watch me," said Ralph. "If I don't get you to the Seaside in ten minutes I give you leave to hand me whatever you think I deserve in the way of punishment. Come on, jump in, and the little 'Gray Ghost' will have you and your baggage at your destination before you know it."

So Tom and Dick jumped into the tonneau with the luggage, while Bert took his seat beside Ralph. Once more they were flying over the road with the wind whistling in their ears to the tune of the throbbing motor. Many nights they had dreamed of it and many days they had talked of it, but to really be there, to feel the mighty power of that great man-made monster, to feel the exhilarated blood come tingling into their faces with the excitement of the race, ah, that was heaven indeed.

But all delightful things must come to an end sometime and so, in the very midst of their enjoyment the speed of the great car slackened and they drew up before a building that looked like an overgrown cottage with a sign in front, announcing to all whom it might concern that this was the "Seaside House." It all looked very comfortable and homelike, and even as they stopped the host advanced to give them welcome.

It took the boys a very short time to explain that they had just come in on the Fearless and only wanted accommodations for a very few days. In less time than it takes to tell the machine was taken around to the garage and the boys had been shown up to two very comfortably furnished rooms.

"Doctor Hamilton expects to stay here, too," Ralph volunteered when they had finished exploring their small domain, "but he won't be able to get here until late this evening. I promised to take the car around for him at the dock about nine o'clock. I suppose all you fellows will go with me, won't you?"

"Surest thing you know," Bert agreed. "I'm glad that he's going to be with us for he knows a lot about the country and he'll go with us on all our expeditions. The Doctor's a jolly good sort."

"He sure is that," said Tom, and so, in the course of time the Doctor arrived and was given the room next to the boys. Just before they went to sleep that night Bert called into Ralph, "Say, Ralph, what do you love best in the world?" and the answer came in three words, "The Gray Ghost."

Next morning bright and early the boys, the Doctor and the "Gray Ghost" started for a visit to Halemaumau, the fire-pit of the crater, Kilauea. The day was ideal for such a trip and the party started off in high spirits. They rode for miles through the most beautiful country they had ever seen until, at last, they came to the foot of the great crater. Only a very few minutes more and they stood within a few yards of the edge of that wonder of wonders, the fire-pit of Kilauea. It is impossible to describe the grandeur of that roaring, surging sea of fire, the tongues of flame lapping one upon another like raging demons in terrific conflict. It is the greatest wonder of Nature ever given to man to witness.

For a few seconds the boys could only stand in amazement that such a thing could be. "If anybody had told me," said Bert, almost whispering in his excitement, "a few months ago that I would be standing here at the edge of the largest living crater in the world, I would have thought that either I was crazy or that they were. I never could forget that sight if I lived forever."

"It sure is about the slickest little bit of Nature that I ever came across," Tom agreed. "If all the scenery is like this we ought to spend four years here instead of a measly four days. I'm beginning to be as much interested in this place as the Doctor is."

"The more you see of it the more you will love it," the Doctor prophesied. "If you would like to we can take a ride across the island to-morrow. It will be about a day's journey, but I can show you a great many points of interest as we go along. What do you say?"

The boys fell in with the plan very readily, and so it was decided that the next morning they would start early. With great reluctance and many backward glances they finally tore themselves away from Halemaumau and turned the "Gray Ghost" toward home. During the ride they could talk of nothing else than the wonder and the magnificent beauty of "The House of Everlasting Fire."

Mile upon mile they rode with the sun filtering through the trees in little golden patches on the road before them, with the caress of the soft breeze upon their faces and the song of the birds in their ears.

"I don't wonder that you think Hawaii's about the nicest place on earth, Doctor," Bert said after a few minutes of silence. "I'm almost beginning to agree with you."

And again the Doctor answered, "The more you see of it the more you will love it."

CHAPTER VI

THE "GRAY GHOST"

The next morning after an early breakfast the "Gray Ghost" was brought around in front of the "Seaside" and the boys began to look her over to make sure that she was in condition for the day's trip. They found that everything was all right, so they began loading her with baskets of delicious eatables that the host had prepared for them. In a very short time all was ready and Tom, Dick and Ralph piled in the tonneau, while the Doctor took his seat beside Bert, who was to drive that day. There had been some discussion that morning as to whether Bert or Ralph were to run the machine. Bert claimed that as it was Ralph's car it was his right and prerogative to drive. But Ralph wouldn't listen to such an argument for a minute. For wasn't Bert his guest and wasn't he there to give his guest a good time, especially as he, Ralph, had driven the car the day before? So after a time it had been settled and Bert reluctantly took the wheel.

But the reluctance didn't last long, for, when he found himself guiding the great car over the road, the old feeling of exultation took possession of him and the old wild desire to put on full speed came surging over him. But Bert was never one to give way to impulse when caution told him it would be unwise, so he held his desire and, incidentally, his machine well in check.

"You said last night that you would tell us about the hunt for sharks, Doctor Hamilton," Dick reminded him. "Won't you tell us about them, now?"

"Why, yes, if you would like to hear about it," the Doctor consented. "These seas, as you probably know, are full of sharks, and therefore are very dangerous. The natives of Hawaii are not the people to be terrorized, however, by any animal on land or sea. So, after careful consideration, they decided that, as long as they couldn't hope to exterminate the pests, the only thing for them to do was to learn how to defend themselves against them. So, when a man wanted to go out into the deep, shark-infested waters he would take with him a handy little dagger. Then, instead of swimming for home and safety at the first sign of a shark, he would wait boldly for the creature to come near enough for a hand-to-hand (or, rather, a fin-to-hand) conflict."

"Say, a man would have to have some nerve to wait calmly while one of those cute, harmless little animals came prancing up playfully to be petted," Tom broke in. "I'd rather be excused."

"It does take an immense amount of courage to brave a shark, but I shouldn't wonder if there were thousands of people in the world who are at this moment making greater sacrifices, performing deeds that call for more real fortitude and courage than these shark hunters ever dreamed of. Only, you see we don't know of those cases. However, that's neither here nor there. Well, to get back to my story, when the shark nears the man he turns on his back to grab him. Then comes the crucial moment. Before the shark has a chance to accomplish his purpose, the native deftly buries the dagger up to the hilt in the shark's throat."

"Yes, but suppose the shark nabbed the hunter before he had a chance to use his weapon," Ralph suggested.

"It is very probable in that case that the hunter would hunt no more sharks," the Doctor laughed. "However, that very rarely happens these days, for the Hawaiians are trained to hunt as soon as they leave the cradle, and are experts at the age of nine or ten."

"I wouldn't mind trying it myself," Bert declared, for, to him danger and excitement were the very breath of life, "only I'd like to practice up for a few years before I hung out my sign."

"Well, they went on killing the sharks by means of a dagger for some time," the Doctor went on, "but one day some bright young native discovered what seemed to him to be a much more interesting and, at the same time, just as sure a way of killing the shark. So one day he called all his relatives and friends together and told them to watch his new method.

They all noticed that, instead of the usual dagger, this youth carried in his hand a pointed stick. 'What good will a sharp stick do?' they all asked one another. 'He surely cannot mean to kill the shark with such a weapon,' and they tried to persuade him not to try anything so foolish. However, he was not to be persuaded, so he started out with his stick to fight the shark. He had not gone very far before his eagerly watching friends on the shore saw a fin rise above the water and knew that the shark was near. With breathless interest they watched the coming conflict. Nearer and nearer came the shark until it was only a very few yards from the daring hunter. Then in a flash it was on its back and bearing down on its prey. With the speed of lightning our hero reached down the shark's throat and wedged the pointed stick right across it so that the shark couldn't close his wicked, gaping mouth. Of course, not being able to shut his mouth he drowned there in his native element. There is an instance of the irony of fate, isn't it?"

"It surely is," Dick answered. "But, Doctor, is that really so or is it only a story?"

"It's the truth. The shark hunters use both methods, the dagger and the sharp stick, but the stick is the favorite."

So the morning was passed in interesting tale and pleasant conversation, and they were all amazed when the Doctor informed them that it was half-past twelve. Soon afterward they came to a cozy little inn with the sign "Welcome" over the door painted in great gold letters on a black background. At this hospitable place they stopped for lunch.

When this most important function of the day was satisfactorily accomplished, they went for a stroll on the beach, as they had about half an hour to look around them before it was necessary to start on their way once more.

This part of the beach was perfectly protected from the unwelcome visits of the sharks by the large coral reefs, and the boys were surprised to see the number of people that were enjoying their afternoon dip.

"Look at those fellows over there riding in on the breakers," Tom cried, pointing to a group of boys that looked as if they might be Americans. "Will you please tell me what they think they have on their feet?"

"They look like snow shoes," Bert said, "but I never knew that you could use skees on the water."

"They are really nothing more nor less than snow shoes, but you see over here they have no snow to use them on, so they make them do for the water," said the Doctor.

"It's a great stunt," said Dick. "I wish we had brought our bathing suits along, we could take a try at it ourselves."

"If bathing suits are all you want," Ralph broke in, "I can soon get you them. This morning I thought we might want them, so, at the last minute, I ran back to get mine. While I was there I discovered your suits all tied together with a strap, so I brought them along, too. They are under the seat in the tonneau."

"Bully for you, old fellow," said Dick. "You have a head on your shoulders, which is more than I can say for myself."

"Yes, that's fine. Now we can try our skill at skeeing on the water. But, by the way, where will we get the skees?"

"They are not really skees; they're only pieces of wood pointed at one end," the Doctor explained, "and I think you will be able to get all you want up at the inn."

"But you will come with us, too, won't you?" Bert asked. "It won't be half as much fun if you don't."

"No, I don't think that I'll go in with you to-day. I brought a little work along, and I thought that if I got a minute I would try to do some of it. You will only have a little while to stay anyway, so go ahead and enjoy yourselves while you may. I'll tell you when time is up. I'll go with you as far as the house. You needn't be afraid that I'll forget."

So, in a few minutes the boys were on the beach once more, ready to try their luck on the skees. They watched the group of fellows that had at first caught their attention until they thought that they knew pretty well what to do. When they fancied they could safely venture they waded out until the water was about to their waists. Then, resting the long board on the water, they tried their best to mount it, as they had seen the other fellows do. But they would just get the board placed nicely with its point toward the shore, when a wave would come along and carry it out from under their feet.

They had very nearly given it up in despair when one of the fellows from the other group came over and spoke to them.

"Is this your first try at the surf boards?" he asked, and they knew from the very tone of his voice that he was what they had thought him, an American. "We saw you were having trouble, and we thought you wouldn't mind if we gave you a few pointers. It's hard to do at first, but when you once catch on it's a cinch."

"We would be very much obliged if you would show us how to manage them," Bert replied. "I thought that I had tried pretty nearly every kind of water trick, but this is a new one on me."

"Yes, we can't seem to get the hang of it," Tom added. "How do you stay on the thing when you once get there?"

So our boys and the others soon became very well acquainted, and it wasn't very long before they were doing as well as the strangers. All too soon they saw the Doctor coming down the beach toward them, and they knew that the time was up. They bade good-bye to their new found friends and hurried up to the inn to get ready for the rest of the journey. For the whole afternoon they rode through scenes of the most striking beauty and grandeur.

They went through the historic valley of Nuuanu, where the great battle was waged by Kamehameha the Great, sometimes called the Napoleon of the Pacific. They followed the scene of that terrible struggle until they came to the precipice over which the Oahu army of more than three thousand men had been forced to a swift death on the rocks below.

When they reached the hotel at which they had expected to stay for the night, they found a telegram waiting for them. Doctor Hamilton opened it and read, "Come at once. Ship sails to-morrow morning, nine o'clock."

"That means," said the Doctor, "that we will have to start for the Fearless as soon as we can get a bite to eat."

So start they did, and it took hard riding nearly the whole night to get them to the ship in time. After they had settled with the landlord of the Seaside House and had hustled their belongings into the car, they started for the dock and found that they were just in the nick of time.

As Bert turned from his companions toward the operating room to take down any last messages that Hawaii might want to send, he said with a sigh, "I'm sorry that we had to leave sooner than we expected, but as long as we had to—say, fellows, wasn't that ride great?"

CHAPTER VII

A SWIM FOR LIFE

It was a hot day, even for the tropics, and everybody felt the heat intensely. Awnings had been stretched over the deck, and under their inviting shade the passengers tried to find relief from the burning sun, but with little success. A slight accident to the machinery had caused the ship to heave to, so that they were deprived of the artificial breeze caused by the vessel's motion. The oppressive heat rivaled anything the boys had ever felt, and for once even their effervescent spirits flagged. They lolled about the deck in listless attitudes, and were even too hot to cut up the usual "monkeyshines" that gave the passengers many a hearty laugh. Dick looked longingly at the green, cool-appearing water, that heaved slowly and rhythmically, like some vast monster asleep.

"Make out it wouldn't feel good to dive in there, and have a good, long swim," he exclaimed, in a wistful voice. "Just think of wallowing around in that cool ocean, and feeling as though you weren't about to melt and become a grease spot at any moment. Gee, I'd give anything I own to be able to jump in right now."

"Go ahead," grinned Bert, "only don't be surprised if we fish you out minus a leg or two. Those two sharks that have been following the ship for the last week would welcome you as a very agreeable addition to their bill of fare."

"Yes," chimed in Ralph, "and that's not the only thing, either. I've felt sorry for those poor old sharks for quite a while. Here they follow our ship around for a week, hoping that somebody will fall overboard and furnish them a square meal, and then everybody disappoints them. I call it pretty mean conduct."

"That's my idea exactly," agreed Bert, "and I think it would only be doing the gentlemanly thing for Dick to volunteer. You won't disappoint your friends on a little point like that, will you, Dick?"

"No, certainly not," responded Dick, scornfully. "Just ring the dinner bell, so that the sharks will be sure not to miss me, and I'll jump in any time you say. Nothing I can think of would give me greater pleasure."

"Well, on second thought," laughed Bert, "I think we'd better save you a little while, and fatten you up. I'm afraid you haven't got fat enough on you at present to give entire satisfaction. We might as well do this thing up right, you know."

"O, sure, anything to oblige," grunted Dick. "Just dispose of me any way you think best. Naturally, the subject has little interest for me."

"Aw, you're selfish, Dick, that's what's the matter with you," said Ralph. "I'd be willing to bet any money that you're thinking more of yourself than you are of those two poor, hungry fish. Gee, I'm glad I'm not like that."

"All right, then," responded Dick, quickly, "as long as you feel that way, and I don't, why don't you serve yourself up to the suffering sharks? Besides, you're fatter than I am."

Apparently Ralph could think of no satisfactory answer to this profound remark and so changed the subject.

"Well," he exclaimed, "all this doesn't get us any nearer to a good swim. I wish this were one of the steamships I was on not long since."

"Why, how was that?" inquired Bert.

"Well, on that ship they had a regular swimming tank on board. Of course, it wasn't a very big one, but it was plenty large enough to give a person a good swim. Gee, I used to just about live in that tank on a day like this."

"I suppose that was what you might call a tank steamer, wasn't it?" said Bert, and his remark raised a general laugh.

But now an elderly man among the passengers, who up to now had listened to the boys' conversation with a smile on his face, but had not spoken, said, "Why don't you ask the captain to rig up the swimming nets?

I'm sure he would be willing to do it for you, if you asked him in the right way."

"Swimming nets!" exclaimed Dick, "what's a swimming net?"

"Why, it's simply a sort of a cage that they rig up alongside the ship, and anybody that wants to can swim to their heart's content inside it. The net keeps sharks out, and makes it safe."

"Say, that would certainly be great," exclaimed Ralph. "Come along, fellows, and we'll see if we can't persuade the captain to fix us up. The idea of a good swim certainly hits me where I live."

The rest were nothing loath, and they jumped to their feet and rushed off in search of Captain Manning. He was soon found, and listened smilingly to Ralph, who acted as spokesman for the others.

"I guess we can arrange that, all right," he said, after Ralph had finished. "It will be at least two hours before our repairs are finished. Between you and me, I'd like to jump in myself," he added, regretfully.

He gave orders accordingly, and the crew soon had the netting rigged. Before they had finished, news of what was going on had flown through the ship. All who felt so disposed or had bathing paraphernalia with them, appeared on deck attired for a dip. Needless to say, Bert, Dick, and Ralph were among the first to put in an appearance, and great was their impatience while the crew were putting the finishing touches to the "cage." While they were waiting, Ralph said, "Look at that, fellows. Those two sharks that we were talking about a little while ago have disappeared. I guess they must have overheard our conversation, and given us up for a bad job."

"They're certainly not in sight, at any rate," said Dick. "However, I think I shall manage to control my grief at their desertion."

"It always gave me a creepy feeling," said the passenger who had first suggested the swimming nets, "they hung on so persistently, just as though they felt sure that their patience would be rewarded some time. It seemed uncanny, somehow."

"It certainly did," agreed another. "I guess they're gone for good, this time, though."

This seemed to be the general opinion among the crew, also, and the boys felt relieved in spite of themselves, for swimming in close proximity to a couple of hungry sharks, even when separated from them by a net, is not a particularly cheerful experience.

Soon everything was ready, and the swimmers descended the steps let down alongside the ship, and plunged into the water. It was very warm, but a good deal cooler than the air, and you may be sure it felt good to the overheated passengers. Bert and Ralph were expert swimmers, and dove and swam in a manner to bring applause from the passengers up above. Dick was not such a very good swimmer, having had little experience in the water. He enjoyed the dip none the less on this account, however, and if he could not swim as well as the others, at least made quite as much noise as they.

After half an hour or so of this the boys ascended to the deck to rest a little before continuing their aquatic exercises.

"My, but that felt good, and no mistake," said Bert.

"It sure did," agreed Ralph. "The only objection I can find is that you can't swim far enough in any one direction. I like to have enough space to let me work up a little speed. I've half a mind to take a chance and dive off here outside the net. There's no sign of those pesky sharks around now. I'm going to take a chance, anyhow," and before anybody had a chance to stop him he had made a pretty dive over the side. He struck the water with scarcely a splash, and in a few seconds rose to the surface and shook the water out of his eyes. Bert yelled at him to come back on board, but he only shook his head and laughed.

Then he struck out away from the ship with bold, rapid strokes, and soon had placed a considerable distance between himself and the vessel. Bert and the others watched his progress with anxious eyes.

"The young fool," growled one of the passengers, "hasn't he got any more sense than to do a thing like that? Those sharks are likely to show up any minute. They don't usually give up so quickly, once they've started to follow a ship."

It seemed, however, as though Ralph would experience no bad results from his rash act. He had swum several hundred yards from the vessel, and had turned to come back, when a cry went up from one of the women passengers.

"Look! Look!" she screamed, and pointed wildly with her parasol. All eyes followed its direction, and more than one man turned white as he looked. For there, not more than five hundred feet from the swimmer, a black fin was cutting the water like a knife-blade. It was not headed directly for Ralph, however, but was going first in one direction, then in another, showing that the shark had not yet definitely located his prey.

A few seconds later a second fin appeared, and there was little doubt in the minds of all that these were the two sharks that had followed the ship for the last few days.

In the meantime, Ralph had drawn nearer the ship, but was swimming in a leisurely fashion, and evidently had no inkling of the deadly peril that threatened him. Bert was about to yell to him and point out his danger, when he thought better of it.

"If he knew those two sharks were on his trail," he said in a strained voice to Tom, "he might get frightened and be unable to swim at all. I think we had better leave him alone and hope that he gets to the ship before the sharks locate him."

"Let's go after him in a boat," suggested one of the sailors, excitedly, and this was no sooner said than done. Without even waiting for orders from the captain, several of the crew started to launch a boat, but it became evident that this could be of no avail. For at that moment the two searching fins suddenly stopped dead for a second, and then started straight for the unconscious swimmer.

A cry went up from the passengers, which reached Ralph's ears. He glanced behind him, and for a second seemed paralyzed at what he saw. Bert yelled wildly. "Swim for your life, Ralph," he shrieked. "Here," turning to the sailors, "get a long rope, and stand by. We'll need it when he gets near the ship."

Now Ralph had recovered from his panic to some extent, and struck out as he had never done before. At every stroke he fairly leaped through the water, but the two black fins overhauled him with lightning-like rapidity. Closer and closer they came, and still the swimmer was a good forty or fifty yards from the ship. Now he started a fast crawl stroke, and it was a lucky thing for him that day that he was an expert swimmer.

He was soon almost under the ship's side, and one of the sailors threw the rope previously secured in his direction. Ralph grasped it with a despairing grip, but now the two fins were terribly close, and approaching at express train speed. A dozen willing hands grasped the rope, and just as the two man-eaters were within ten feet of him the exhausted swimmer was swung bodily out of the water. There was a swish alongside, two great white streaks flashed by, and the passengers caught a glimpse of two horrible, saw-like rows of gleaming teeth. Then Ralph was drawn up on a level with the rail, and strong hands pulled him safely inboard.

No sooner did he realize that he was safe, than he collapsed, and it was some time before he recovered from the strain. When he was once more himself, he grinned weakly at Bert. "Next time I'll follow your advice," he said.

"Oh, well, 'all's well that ends well,'" quoted Bert. "Just the same, it was more than you deserved to have us work ourselves to death a hot day like this trying to keep you from doing the Jonah act. It would have served you right if we had let the shark take a bite or two."

"Sorry to have troubled you, I'm sure," retorted Ralph. "But say, fellows, just as soon as I can get enough nerve back to think, I'm going to dope out some way of getting even with those man-eaters. I'll be hanged if I'm going to let even a shark think he can try to make hash of me and get away with it. In the meantime, you and Tom might set your giant intellects to work and see if you can think of a plan."

A sailor had overheard this, and now he touched his cap, and said:

"Excuse me for buttin' in, but I think me and my mates here can fix up those sharks for you, if the captain's willin'. On a bark I sailed in once we caught a shark that had been annoyin' us like these has, just like you'd catch a fish. We baited a big hook, and pulled him in with the donkey engine. If the captain ain't got no objections, I don't see why we couldn's sarve these lubbers the same trick."

This idea met with instant approval, and Captain Manning was soon besieged by a fire of entreaty. At first he seemed inclined to say no, but when he found that the majority of the passengers were in favor of capturing the sharks, he gave a reluctant consent.

The sailors grinned in happy anticipation of a good time, and set about their preparations with a will, while an interested group that surrounded them watched the development of their scheme with intense interest.

CHAPTER VIII

THE CAPTURED SHARK

The species of shark that inhabits tropical waters is very voracious, and will eat almost anything that has the smell or taste of food about it. Therefore, the sailors were troubled by no fears that the bait they were preparing would not prove tempting enough.

The cook had provided them with a huge slab of salt pork, and then the problem arose as to what they could use as a hook. Finally, however, one of the sailors unearthed a large iron hook, such as is used on cranes and other hoisting machinery. The point of this was filed down until it was sharp as a needle, and the big piece of meat was impaled on it.

"That ought to hook one of them blarsted man-hunters," remarked one grizzled old sea dog, who was known to his companions as "Sam," and apparently had no other name. "If that hook once gets caught in his gizzard, we'll have him on board unless the rope breaks, won't we mates?"

"Aye, aye. That we will," came in a gruff chorus from the bronzed and hardy crew, and matters began to look dark for the unconscious sharks.

When the meat had been securely tied to the hook, the big crane used to store the cargo in the hold was brought into use, and the hook made fast to the end of the strong wire cable.

"Gee," said Tom, who had been regarding these preparations with a good deal of interest, as indeed had everybody on deck, "I begin to see the finish of one of those beasts, anyway. I can see where we have shark meat hash for the rest of this voyage, if the cook ever gets hold of him."

"Oh, they're not such bad eating, at that," said Ralph. "Why, when once in a while one becomes stranded on the beach and the natives get hold of him, they have a regular feast day. Everybody for miles around is notified, and they troop to the scene of festivities by the dozen. Then they build fires, cut up the shark, and make a bluff at cooking the meat before they start to eat it. But you can hardly call it eating. They fairly gorge it, and sometimes eat steadily a whole day, or at any rate until the shark is all gone but his bones. Then they go to bed and sleep off the results of their feed. They don't need anything else to eat for some days."

"Heavens, I shouldn't think they would, after that," laughed Bert. "I think if I ate a whole day without stopping it would end my worldly career at once. Subsequent events wouldn't have much interest for me."

"Oh, well," said Dick, in a whimsical tone, "I suppose they think if they did die, they would at least have died happy."

"And full," supplemented Bert.

"Oh, that's the same thing with them," laughed Ralph. "That's their idea of paradise, I guess. They're always happy when they have enough to eat, anyway."

"Well, that's the way with all of us, isn't it?" asked Dick. "You're never very happy when you're hungry, I know that."

"But there's a shark not very far from here that's not going to be very happy when he's eaten a square meal that we're going to provide him," laughed Bert, and the others agreed with him.

By this time everything was ready for the catching of at least one of the sharks, and steam was turned into the engine operating the crane. The machine proved to be in first-class condition, and so the baited hook was carried to the side and slowly eased into the water. An empty cask had previously been tied to it, however, to act as a float, and all eyes were fastened eagerly on this. It drifted slowly away from the ship's side, as the cable was paid out, and was checked when it had reached a distance of perhaps a hundred and fifty feet from the vessel.

The sailors had armed themselves with axes and clubs, and waited expectantly for the disturbance around the cask that would show when the monster had been hooked.

For some time, however, the cask floated serenely, without even a ripple disturbing it. Many were the disappointed grumblings heard among passengers and crew, but the confidence of old Sam was not shaken.

"Give him time, give him time!" he exclaimed. "You don't expect him to come up and swally the bait right on scratch, like as though he was paid to do it, do ye? Have a little patience about ye, why don't ye? Bein' disappointed in takin' a nip out of the lad, there, them sharks will hang around, hoping for another chanst, never fear. Time ain't money with them fellers."

The words were scarcely out of his mouth when the cask disappeared in a whirl of foam, and a cheer arose from the spectators. The steel cable whipped up out of the water, and sprang taut as a fiddle string. The big crane groaned as the terrific strain came upon it.

"Say, but that must be a big fellow," exclaimed Bert, in an excited voice. "Just look at that cable, will you. It takes some pull to straighten it out like that."

But now the shark, seeming to realize that he could not get away by pulling in one direction, suddenly ceased his efforts, and the cable slackened. Captain Manning gave the signal to the engineer to start winding in the cable, but hardly had the drum of the crane started to revolve, when the shark made a great circular sweep in a line almost parallel with the ship. The cable sang as it whipped through the water in a great arc, and the whole ship vibrated to the terrific strain.

But the great fish was powerless against the invincible strength of steam, and was slowly drawn to the ship as revolution after revolution of the inexorable engine drew in the cable. Leaning breathlessly over the side, the passengers and crew could gradually make out the shape of the struggling, lashing monster as he was drawn up to the ship's side. He made short dashes this way and that in a desperate effort to break away, but all to no purpose. When he was right under the ship's side, but still in the water, the captain ordered the engine stopped, and requested the passengers to retire to a safe distance. Bert, Dick, and Ralph pleaded hard to be allowed to take a hand in dispatching the monster, but Captain Manning was inexorable, and they were forced to withdraw from the scene of the coming struggle.

The crew grasped their weapons firmly, and as one put it, "cleared for action."

Then the signal was given to resume hoisting the big fish aboard, and once more the crane started winding up the cable. Slowly, writhing and twisting, the shark was hauled up the side. He dealt the ship great blows with his tail, any one of which would have been sufficient to kill a man. His smooth, wet body gleamed in the sun's rays, and his wicked jaws snapped viciously, reminding the spectators of the teeth of some great trap. All his struggles were in vain, however, and finally, with one great "flop" he landed on the deck.

He lashed out viciously with his powerful tail, and it would have been an ill day for any member of the crew that inadvertently got in its path. Needless to say, they were very careful to avoid this, and dodged quickly in and out, dealing the monster heavy blows whenever the opportunity offered. Slowly his struggles grew less strong, and at last he lay quite still, with only an occasional quiver of his great carcass. Then old Sam stepped quickly in, and delivered the "coup de grace" in the form of a stunning blow at the base of the shark's skull.

This was the finishing blow, and soon the passengers were allowed to gather around and inspect the dead monster. A tape-measure was produced, and it was found that the shark was exactly twelve feet and seven inches long.

"Why," remarked Dick, "you'd have been nothing but an appetizer to this fellow, if he had caught you, Ralph. He sure is some shark."

"Well, I won't contradict you," said Ralph, "but I don't think this shark was the same one that chased me. Why, it seems to me that that fellow was nothing but teeth. That's all I remember noticing, at any rate."

"Yes, but this rascal seems to have quite a dental outfit," said Dick. "Just think what it must be to a shark if he starts to get a toothache in several teeth at once. It must be awful."

"I'm certainly glad our teeth aren't quite as numerous," laughed Bert. "Just think of having to have a set of false teeth made. A person would have to work about all his lifetime to pay for a set like that."

"It would be fine for the dentists, though," remarked Ralph, but then he added, "I wonder what they're going to do with this fellow, now that they've caught him."

"Throw him overboard, I suppose," said Bert. "I don't think he's of much use to us, seeing that we're not like the savages Ralph was telling us about."

And that is just about what they did do. First, however, the sailors secured a number of the shark's teeth, and these were distributed among the passengers as souvenirs. Then the great carcass was hoisted up until it dangled over the water, and the hook was cut out. The dead monster struck the water with a splash, and slowly sank from view.

"Well, Ralph, now you've had your revenge, anyway," said Bert. "I don't think there's much doubt that that was one of the pair that came so near to ending your promising career. He looked to be about the same size as the one that almost had you when we hauled you out."

"Oh, I guess it's the same one, all right," agreed Ralph, "and I owe everyone a vote of thanks, I guess. I hope I never come quite so near a violent death again. It was surely a case of nip and tuck."

The crew now set to work to clear up the mess that had been made on the deck, and soon all mementoes of the bloody struggle were removed. Shortly afterward the chief engineer reported that the break in the machinery had been repaired, and it was not very long before the ship renewed its interrupted voyage.

At the dinner table that night little else was spoken of, and Ralph was congratulated many times on his lucky escape.

And one of the passengers voiced the general sentiment, when he said with a smile that "he was satisfied if the ship broke down often, provided they always had as exciting an experience as they had had to-day."

CHAPTER IX

IN THE HEART OF THE TYPHOON

Over the quiet ocean so calm that, except for an occasional swelling foam-tipped wave it seemed like a sea of glass, the noon-day sun poured its golden light. It was a perfect day at sea, and so thought the passengers on board the swift ocean greyhound that plowed its way through the quiet waters of the Pacific.

A stately ship was she, a palace upon the waves. No deprivation here of any comfort or luxury that could be found on land. Her shining brass work gleamed in the sunshine like molten gold. The delicate colors in her paneling blended with the tints of the soft rugs on her polished floors. On deck, in the saloons, and staterooms, all was luxury. Gay groups of passengers, richly dressed, paraded her decks or lay at ease in their steamer chairs, or upon the softly-upholstered couches and divans of her gorgeous saloons. Japanese servants glided noiselessly to and fro, ministering to the slightest wish of these favored children of fortune. Everywhere were signs of wealth and ease and careless gaiety. Sounds of music and merry laughter floated over the quiet waters. Pain, fear, suffering, disaster, danger, death,—what had such words as these to do with this merry company? If anyone had mentioned the possibility of peril, of calamity, the idea would have been scouted. Why, this great ship was as safe as any building on land. Was it not fitted with water-tight compartments? Even such an unlikely thing as a collision could bring no fatal catastrophe.

That this feeling of absolute security is felt by all can be very plainly seen. Go to the perfectly appointed smoking-room and scan the faces of the gentlemen, quietly smoking and reading, or talking in friendly fashion together, or enjoying a game of cards. Every face is serene.

Pass on into the music-room. A waltz is being played by the piano and violin, and gay couples of young people are enjoying the dance to the utmost. Groups of interested older people look on with smiles. No anxiety here. Nothing but happy, care-free faces.

But come into the captain's private cabin where he is standing, listening earnestly to one of his officers. Perfect appointments here also, but evidently they do not appeal to these men at this moment. No smiles of gaiety here. The captain's face pales as he listens to his officer's words.

"The barometer has fallen several inches in the last hour and a half," was the announcement. Not enough in this, one may think, to cause anxiety. But the captain knew and realized, as few on board beside himself could, that the ship was nearing the coast of Japan, the latitude most frequently visited by the dreaded typhoon, and also that this mid-summer season was the most dangerous time of the year.

Among the first signs of danger from one of these terrible visitors is an unusually rapid fall of the barometer. No wonder that, with the responsibility of the lives and safety of hundreds of people resting upon him, his face should blanch with apprehension.

Verifying his officer's statement by a quick look at the barometer, he went hastily on deck. Here his quick eye noticed the change in weather conditions; not very great as yet, only a slight cloudiness which dimmed the brightness of the sun. Not enough to trouble the passengers who, if they noticed it at all, were only conscious of an added sense of comfort in the softening of the almost too brilliant sunshine, but enough to deepen the pallor of the captain's face and quicken his pulse with the realization of a great, impending danger. Even as he looked the heavens began still more to darken, the clouds increased in size and blackness and began to move wildly across the sky. The wind freshened and the quiet sea broke into billowswhich grew larger and more angry-looking each passing moment.

Taking his stand on the bridge, the captain summoned all his officers to him and gave quick, decisive orders. With the rapidity of lightning his orders are executed and soon everything is made snug. Every possible measure is taken to safeguard the ship.

But, now it was evident to all that more than an ordinary storm threatened them. In an almost incredibly short time the whole aspect of sky and sea had changed. The surface of the ocean was lashed into mountainous waves which raced before the terrible wind. The heavens darkened until an almost midnight blackness settled down over the appalled voyagers.

Vanished are the sounds of music and laughter. Gone the happy, care-free look from the faces. Filled with terror, they awaited they knew not what. The wind increased, and now the heavens opened and the rain came in such a torrential downpour that it seemed almost as if the great, staunch ship would be beaten beneath the waves.

With a feeling of agonized despair, the captain realized that that which he so feared had come upon the vessel, and that she was in the grasp of the dreaded typhoon. The darkness thickened, the wind increased, and suddenly they felt themselves caught in a great wave which tossed the ship about like a child's toy. Back and forth twisted the great ship, completely at the mercy of this remorseless wind and sea.

Thunderous crashing was heard as the upper works of the ship were torn away by the gigantic waves that washed over her. The passengers were panic-stricken and rushed wildly about, seeking those who were dear to them, their cries and groans drowned in the roaring of tumultuous seas. The captain, calm and self-controlled in the midst of this terrible scene, went about among them, restraining, soothing, speaking words of encouragement and hope, but in his heart he had no hope. A fireman rushed up with the report that the engine-rooms were flooded and the fires out; and then, with blows that made the great ship tremble, part of timbers were torn away by the great seas which made no more of iron girders or sheets of riveted steel than if they were strips of cardboard. The sea rushed in from more than one jagged opening in her side.

Now at last, the captain realized that his splendid ship was doomed. The great vessel was slowly sinking. One hour, a little more, a little less, would see the end. And, to make their doom more certain, he could not launch a single life-boat for they had all been shattered and washed away by the sea. There is but one hope left, and quickly ascertaining that the wireless is still O. K., the captain orders the call for help. For who can tell at what moment the apparatus might be disabled? Eagerly the operator bends above his key and forth across the angry waves, defying the forces of wind and wave and torrent that have sought to cut them off from all succor, goes that pitiful cry for help.

With every nerve strained to the utmost tension he awaits the response that will assure him that his call is heard and that help is coming; but, before his ear can catch the welcome signal a flash, a whirring and snapping, tells him that the apparatus has gone dead! They must wait for the weary danger-fraught moments to bring them the knowledge. Thank God the cry for help was sent in time. There is a chance of its reaching some ship near enough to rescue them; but near indeed that ship must be or she will bring help too late.

Twenty miles away the good ship Fearless plows through mountainous billows that, breaking, drench her decks with spray.

In his wireless room Bert is sitting with his receiver at his ear on the alert for any message. His three chums are with him as usual, Tom and Ralph sitting in a favorite attitude with arms across the back of a chair in front of them, while Dick walked excitedly up and down the room. Quite a difficult task he found that for the ship was rolling considerably. As he walked he talked.

"Well, fellows," he was saying, "I have always wanted to see a genuine storm at sea, and to-day I think I've seen it."

"It seems to me that you've seen a great deal more storm to-day than you longed for or ever care to see again," Tom commented.

"You're just right there," Dick agreed. "It would be all right if you could watch the storm without sharing the danger. There was one time this afternoon when I thought it was certainly all over with us."

"It sure did look that way, and I guess Captain Manning thought so, too," Tom said.

"It was a lucky thing for the Fearless," Ralph broke in, "that the storm didn't last long. If it had kept on much longer we shouldn't be here talking about it now."

"But wasn't Captain Manning fine through it all?" said Bert.

They were all feeling the effects of one of the most thrilling experiences of their lives.

The Fearless, fortunate in not being in the direct course of the typhoon, had felt its force sufficiently to place her in great danger and to make every man Jack of her crew do his duty in a desperate effort to keep his ship from going to the bottom. That they had come through safely with no greater damage than the washing away of her life-boats was largely due to Captain Manning's strength and courage, and the young fellows were filled with admiration. Each in his heart had resolved to prove himself as brave if a time of trial should come to him.

With this thought in mind they had sat very quietly for a few moments after Bert's last remark, but now they all thrilled with a new excitement as Bert suddenly straightened up from his lounging position, and, with kindling eye and every faculty alert, grasped the key of his instrument. The others knew that he had caught a wireless message and feared from the sudden flushing and paling of his face that it was a call for help.

In the twinkling of an eye all was again excitement on board the Fearless. The ship's course was altered and, with full steam pressure on her engines, she fairly flew to the rescue. Twenty miles, and a trifle over fifty minutes to reach that sinking ship. Could she make it? Hearts felt and lips asked the question as the Fearless raced over the water, and all eyes were strained in a vain effort to catch a sight of the ship to whose succor they were going long before there was even the remotest possibility of sighting her. Their own peril was so recently passed that all on board the Fearlessthrobbed with pity for those so much more unfortunate than themselves, and prayed heaven that they might be in time.

But if eyes were strained on the Fearless, how much more earnestly did everyone of those on the ill-fated steamer look for some sign or sound from a rescuing ship? The typhoon had passed very quickly, but what havoc it had wrought in so short a time! The floating palace that had seemed so secure was now reduced to a dismantled, twisted hulk, water-logged and slowly carrying her unfortunate passengers to destruction.

A whole hour had passed since the message had been sent forth to seek and find help, but no help had come. Who shall attempt to record the history of that hour? At first hope, faint it is true but still hope, then increasing anxiety as the doomed vessel settled deeper and deeper in the water, then growing despair as all feared, what the captain and crew knew, that in a very little while would come the end. Even if a vessel should appear now, the captain feared that only a few could be saved, as it must be a work of time to transfer those hundreds of passengers from one ship to another. As all the life-boats had been smashed and carried away, precious minutes must be lost awaiting a boat from the rescuing ship. But in order that all might be in readiness, the women and children were placed close to the rail to be taken first, and the other passengers told off in squads for each succeeding embarkation so that there need be no confusion at the last moment.

To the poor unfortunates those long minutes of waiting, fraught with possibilities of life or death, had seemed like hours. A great quiet had fallen over them, the paralyzing stupor of despair. Nearly all had ceased to hope or look for rescue, but sat with bowed heads, awaiting the fate which could not now be long delayed.

Suddenly, through this silent despairing company ran an electric thrill. Life pulsed in their veins, and hope that they had thought dead, sprang anew in their hearts. A sailor casting one despairing glance about him, had seen the smokestacks of a steamer gleaming red through the faint mist that still hung over the water. Springing to his feet, he began shouting, "Sail ho! a sail! a sail!" For a moment all was wildest confusion, and it was with greatest difficulty that the captain, who had prepared for just this outbreak, could control these frantic people and restore discipline among them. By this time, the lookout on the Fearless had made out the wreck and a heartening toot-toot from her steam whistle gladdened the waiting hundreds. But would she reach them in time? Already the captain had noticed the trembling of the ship that so surely foretells the coming plunge into the depths of the ocean. It is a miracle that Fate had so long stayed her hand. To be lost now, with life and safety almost within their grasp, would be doubly terrible.

Breathlessly they wait until the steamer moving at the very limit of her speed, comes nearer and nearer, till at last she slows and drifts only a few hundred feet away.

To the surprise of the Fearless, no attempt was made on board the sinking ship to lower her boats; and equal was the consternation on board the sinking steamer, when they saw that no boats were lowered from the other ship.

"Her boats are gone, too," shouted Bert as the situation became plain to all. No sooner had the words left his lips than the Fearless' carpenters were at work, and in an incredibly short space of time, a rough life buoy was knocked together. They worked with a will for they knew that every second might mean a life. The buoy consisted of a rude platform with uprights at its four corners, to the top of each of which a pulley was securely fastened. Around the uprights ropes were wound making a rude but safe conveyance.

While this was doing, a ball with string attached was shot from a small cannon on board the Fearless. Whistling through the air, it landed just within the wrecked ship's rail. Eager hands prevent it from slipping and there is no lack of helpers to draw in the line to the deck. With deft but trembling hands the crew work to secure the cable which follows the line.

At last the life line is adjusted and secured between the two ships, the life buoy comes speeding over the water to the doomed vessel, and as it rushed back toward the waiting Fearless, with its load of women and children, a great cheer goes up. A moment, and the forlorn creatures are lifted by tender hands to the Fearless, and the buoy swings back for a second load. The work of rescue has begun.

Back and forth swings the buoy until the women and children are all safe, and still the miracle holds; the wreck still floats. In less time than would have seemed possible, all the sufferers from the wreck have reached the rescuing ship except the captain and his first mate, and the life buoy is swung back for the last time. Hurry now, willing hands! Already the bow of the sinking steamer is buried beneath the waves. Another moment or two, and it will be too late. Only a few feet more. Speed, speed, life buoy! She reaches the rail. Eager hands draw the two last voyagers over and cut the now useless life line. As the men step to the deck of the Fearless the wreck, with one more convulsive shiver, plunges to her last resting place, but, thank God, with not one soul left upon her. All are saved, and Bert, overcome, bows his head upon his arms, and again thanks heaven for the wireless. Once more it has wrought a miracle and plucked a host of precious lives from the maw of the ravenous sea.

CHAPTER X

THE DERELICT

"Beat this if you can, fellows," said Tom, as, next morning, lazily stretched in his steamer chair on the deck of the Fearless, his eyes took in with delight the broad expanse of the ocean, with its heaving, green billows, capped with feathery foam of dazzling whiteness; the arching blue of the heavens, across which floated soft, gray clouds, which, pierced through and through by the brilliant sunshine, seemed as transparent as a gossamer veil. A sea-gull, rising suddenly from the crest of a wave, soared high with gracefully waving wings; then suddenly turning, swooped downward with the speed of an arrow, disappearing for a moment beneath the wave, rose again, triumphant, with a fish in its talons, and swept majestically skyward.

Fountains of spray cast up by the swiftly moving ship gleamed and flashed in the sunshine and fell to the deck in myriad diamonds.

Tom's pleasure was fully shared by his comrades, and surely in contrast to the storm and stress and darkness of yesterday, the sunshine and calm and beauty of this matchless day was enough to fill them with keenest delight. The swift motion of the good ship that had so gallantly weathered the terrible storm, the sea air which, freighted with salt spray as it rushed against their faces made the flesh tingle, the brilliant sunshine,—all combined to make this one of the happiest mornings of their lives.

From sheer exuberance of joy Dick started singing

"A life on the ocean wave,"

in which the others joined. As the last notes died away they began to talk of yesterday's storm. Something that Tom said reminded Dick of an exciting sea story he had read, and, complying with Tom's eager "Tell us about it," he was soon in the midst of the yarn, the boys listening with eager delight. Others, seeing their absorbed interest, drifted up until Dick had quite an audience of interested listeners.

This story was followed by others, and one of the passengers had just finished describing the very narrow escape of a boatload of sailors who were being drawn to destruction by the dying struggles of an enormous whale which they had harpooned, when Bert, who, while he listened, had been idly watching a sail which had appeared above the horizon, suddenly sprang to his feet in great excitement and drew everybody's attention.

"What is it? what is it?" cried Tom, catching the excitement and also springing to his feet.

"Why," Bert answered, "look at that ship to starboard. I've been watching her for some time and she acts differently from any ship I ever saw. At first she seemed to be sailing a little distance and then back again in a sort of zig-zag course, but just a minute ago she turned side-on toward us, and now she looks as if she were veering from one point of the compass to another without any attempt at steering."

Following his gaze, all saw with intense surprise the ship, as Bert had said, apparently without guidance and drifting aimlessly.

After the first moments of startled silence, exclamations and questions broke forth on all sides.

"Well, well, what a most extraordinary thing!" "What ship can she be?" "She looks like a schooner." "Why does she drift in that aimless fashion?" "What can be the matter with her?"

By this time glasses had been brought. Eager eyes scanned the strange ship from stem to stern, and one of the gazers exclaimed:

"She certainly doesn't seem to have anyone at her wheel. She is evidently at the mercy of the sea."

This set everyone to talking at once and the greatest excitement reigned. Everyone crowded to the side of the ship to get a better view. The stranger seemed to be about three miles away, but, as the distance lessened between her and the Fearless, the excitement on board increased, and as, even with the glasses, no sign of living creature could be seen, the sense of mystery deepened.

When, at last, the captain announced that he would send a boat out to speak the strange ship, a murmur of satisfaction was heard on every side. At the call for volunteers there was no lack of response and our boys were among them.

It was with breathless delight that they heard their names called, and tumbled with others into the boat.

"Here's luck," Dick exulted as he scrambled to his place. The others agreed with him. But, if they had expected a pleasure trip, they were quickly undeceived. Standing on the deck of a great ship like the Fearless is a very different thing from sitting in a small boat, with the waves which, from the ship's deck had looked only moderately large, now piling up into a great, green wall in front of them, looking as if it must inevitably fall upon and crush them.

That the wave did not conquer them, but that the boat mounted to the top of it, seemed little short of a miracle; and then, after poising for a moment at the top, the plunge down the other side of that green wall, seemed an equally sure way to destruction. They were glad indeed to remember that the boat was in the hands of experienced and capable seamen. Altogether, they were not sorry when, by the slowing up of the speed, they knew that they were nearing their goal and saw the ship that had so interested them looming up before them.

Her name, The Aurora, flashed at them in great golden letters from her prow. She was a fair-sized schooner in first-class condition outwardly, and calling for a crew of eighteen or twenty beside the captain and officers; but, where were they now? Sure enough, there was no one at the wheel nor anywhere about the decks. Were they below? If so, what was the desperate need or urgent business that could hold officers and crew below decks while their ship, unguarded, her rudder banging noisily back and forth, lay, uncontrolled, upon the waves?

Well, they from the Fearless were here to answer these questions if they could, and preparations were made to go on board. As they drew closer they realized that it was going to be a very difficult task to gain her deck. With the wheel unmanned she broached to and fro with every current and wave motion, and, constantly veering from point to point, made it seemingly impossible to mount her decks. A little assistance from on board would have helped them greatly, but, though they hailed her again and again, she made no response.

After repeated unsuccessful efforts one of the sailors, more agile than the others, succeeded in springing into and grasping the rudder chains, and hauling himself on deck. Catching up a rope that lay near him, he cast it to his shipmates and, by easing and adjusting the boat as much as possible to the erratic heaving and plunging of the ship, made it possible for the others to climb on board. Very soon all, except two sailors who, much to their disgust, were left in charge of the boat, were standing together on the steamer's deck.

With bated breath they stood for many minutes, looking about them in wide-eyed amazement, but, as if by common instinct, not an audible sound was heard, nor even a whispered word. A silence so intense as to make itself felt, a sense of overwhelming loneliness and solitude held them motionless. It was as if they stood in the presence of the dead. Here was the body, this big schooner, but the soul had fled. The rush of feet, the quick word of command, the hearty "Aye, aye, sir," in response, the noise of gear and tackle, of ropes slapping on the deck, the songs of the sailors as they go lustily about their work,—all the sounds that make up the life of a ship were stilled, and no sound but the splashing of the waves against her sides broke the awesome silence.

At last, under the direction of Mr. Collins, four men from the Fearless began to search the deck for some solution of the mystery, and not one among them was conscious of the fact that he moved about on his toes in the presence of this awe-inspiring silence.

Their search of the deck revealed nothing. Everything seemed undisturbed. The life-boats and even the little dinghy were in their places. All was perfectly ship-shape, but over everything was the silence of desertion.

While the deck was being searched by the four men, the others, including Bert and Dick and Tom, went below, for, here in the cabin, they hoped to find some solution of the mystery. But again they found the same chilling silence, the same absolute desertion.

In the state-rooms the bunks were made up and all was in order. An uncompleted letter lay on the captain's table and an open book lay face-downward on the bed. In the cabin the only sign of haste or disturbance was found. The table was set for breakfast with the food upon it only partly eaten. Chairs were pushed back from it and one was overturned. A handkerchief lay on the floor as if hastily dropped, but there was no further sign of panic or of any struggle.

Someone suggested that the storm had driven them away in panic. Mr. Collins soon proved to them the fallacy of that supposition by calling attention to an unfinished garment which lay on a sewing machine in one of the state-rooms. A thimble and spool of cotton lay beside it. In a storm these things would inevitably have been thrown to the floor. He showed them further that the breakfast things on the table were in their places and not overturned as they must have been in the storm. Then, too, the coffee in the urn was barely cold, and the fire in the galley stove was still burning. This proved conclusively that up to almost the last moment before the desertion of the ship, all was normal and peaceful on board. "And," he continued, "if there were nothing else the last entry in the ship's log would show that she was not deserted until after the storm."

While everyone listened with keenest interest, he read them the account entered there of the storm, the gallant behavior of the Aurora, and the safety of all on board. The entry was made with the kind of ink that writes blue but afterwards turns black, and the officer called their attention to the fact that the ink was not yet black.

"Why," said he, "they must at this moment be only a very few miles from the ship. Did anyone ever hear of anything like this?" wondered Dick. "Such a little while ago, and absolutely nothing to show why they went. I'd give a whole lot to know."

"Well, anyway, it is evident," said Bert as they examined the galley, "that it was not hunger or thirst that drove them away," and he pointed to the shelves of the pantry, well stocked with meats and vegetables and fruits, and lifted the cover from the water tank and showed it full of sweet water.

With the feeling of wonder and amazement growing upon them, they examined every corner of the ship from deck to hold, but found no sign of living creature, nor any clue to the profound mystery. Cold shivers began to run up and down their spines.

"What on earth or sea," said the irrepressible Tom, voicing the inmost thought of every mind, "could have driven a company of men to abandon a ship in such perfect condition as this schooner is?" and again all stood silent in a last effort to solve the problem.

"Well," said Mr. Collins, "we have made a most thorough search and nothing can be gained by remaining here longer." So, only waiting to procure the ship's log that he had laid upon the table, he led the way to the deck. With a last look about them, in the vain hope of finding some living creature, they clambered into the boat and rowed back to the Fearless.

On the way over, everyone was too oppressed for further conversation, but as they neared the Fearless their faces brightened; and as they stood once more upon her decks, with the eager people crowding about them, it seemed good, after the desolation they had witnessed, to be on board a live ship once more.

"This is surely a most wonderful and mysterious thing," said the captain, after listening to their report. "What could have driven them to such a desperate measure as abandoning a ship in sound condition and so well provisioned? Was it mutiny?"

"No, sir," and the mate shook his head. "I thought of that and we searched the ship for any signs of a struggle or bloodshed; but there was no evidence of fighting nor a drop of blood anywhere."

"Was there, perhaps, a leak?" again suggested the captain.

"Not that we could find," Dick answered. "The ship seemed as tight and safe as could be. We are sure there is no leak."

"What do you think about it?" asked Captain Manning, turning to a very grave and thoughtful gentleman standing near. This was Captain Grant who the day before had so nobly stood by his ill-fated ship and to whose rescue and that of his unfortunate passengers the Fearless had come with not a minute to spare. Captain Manning had found him very congenial, and in the few hours since he had come on board the two gentlemen had become firm friends. At Captain Manning's question he turned to him cordially and answered with a smile:

"Well, as far as the crew are concerned, it might have been superstition, fear of ghosts perhaps. This unreasoning fear has driven more than one crew bodily from their ship."

"If that was the cause," ventured Bert, "is it not possible that their panic may leave them, and that they may return?"

"It is possible," agreed Captain Manning, smiling, "and we will cruise about as soon as I can make preparation. We may be able to overtake them or perhaps meet them returning."

"Was her cargo a valuable one?" asked one of Captain Grant's passengers.

"Yes, quite," was the response, "but not so valuable as it would have been if she had been homeward instead of outward bound. The log shows her to be of Canadian construction and bound from Vancouver to China with a cargo of dried fish, skins, and lumber. If she had been returning she would have been freighted, as you know, with rich silks and tea and rice, of more value than the cargo she carried from British Columbia."

"Shall you attempt to return her to her owners?" asked Mr. Collins. "A schooner like the Aurora would mean a large salvage."

"It certainly would," replied the captain, "and, if we had found her earlier in the voyage, I should have towed her back. But now I cannot afford the time, and I hardly know what to do. She ought not to be left drifting; she is right in the track of steamships, and so is a menace. Wilson," he said, turning to Bert, "try to raise a United States vessel and give her the location of the derelict."

It took two hours before Bert succeeded, but at last he reached the cruiser Cormorant and received thanks for the information and assurance that the matter would be attended to at once.

By this time all was ready and the Fearless began to cruise in ever-widening circles around the Aurora. With and without glasses all scanned the sea in every direction for signs of a boat. Once the call of the lookout drew all eyes to a dark object which, at that distance, looked as if it might be a yawl, and every heart beat faster with the hope that at last the mystery of the Aurora might be solved. But, alas, it was found to be only a piece of broken mast, discarded from some ship.

For several hours they cruised about, filled with eager hope which gradually faded as the hours went by. At last, Captain Manning gave the order, and the Fearless again came about to her course.

Everyone turned disappointedly from the rail as the quest was abandoned, and it seemed to the four young fellows that the Fearless swung slowly and reluctantly, as if she disliked to leave her sister ship to such an uncertain fate.

The good ship gathered speed, and as they stood at the rail, Ralph thoughtfully said, "I wonder if the mystery of that deserted ship will ever be made clear."

"Well," said Bert, "when we return we can ascertain if she lived to reach port."

"Yes," grumbled Tom. "But unless some of the crew had returned before the government ship reached her the mystery would be as profound as ever. And," he added, sinking disgustedly into his steamer chair, and stretching himself out lazily, "I do hate mysteries."

CHAPTER XI

THE TIGER AT BAY

One day, about mid-afternoon, Bert was going through his duties in a more or less mechanical fashion, for the day had been warm, and he had been on duty since early morning. For several days past, practically no news of any interest had come in over the invisible aerial pathways, and as he had said to Dick only a short time before, "everything was deader than a door nail."

Suddenly, however, the sounder began to click in a most unusual fashion. The clicks were very erratic, quick, and short, and to Bert's experienced ear it was apparent that the person sending the message was in a state of great excitement. He hastily adjusted the clamp that held the receiver to his ear, and at the first few words of the message his heart leapt with excitement.

"Tiger broken loose," came the message, in uneven spurts and dashes, "three of crew dead or dying—am shut up in wireless room—beast is sniffing at door—help us if you can—" and then followed, latitude and longitude of the unlucky vessel.

Bert's hand leaped to the sender, and the powerful spark went crashing out from the wires. "Will come at once—keep up courage," he sent, and then snatched the apparatus off his head and rushed in mad haste to the deck. Captain Manning was below deck, and Bert communicated the message he had just received to the commanding officer at the time.

"Good heavens," ejaculated the first officer, "there's only one thing for us to do, and that's to go to their aid just as fast as this old tub will take us."

This was no sooner said than done, and in a few minutes the course of the vessel was changed, and she was headed in the direction of the distressed animal ship, for there could be little doubt that such was the nature of the cargo she had on board. It is not such an uncommon thing for a wild animal to break loose during a voyage, but generally it is recaptured with little trouble. Occasionally, however, an especially ferocious animal will escape, and at the very outset kill or maim the men especially employed to take care of them. Once let this happen, and the crew has little chance against such an enemy. Nothing much more terrible could be imagined than such a situation, and such was the plight in which the crew of the animal ship found themselves. They had made several vain attempts to trap the big tiger, but at each attempt one of their number had been caught and killed by the ferocious beast, until in a panic they had retreated to the forecastle, taking with them the first mate, who had been seriously injured by the murderous claws of the tiger as they were trying to cast a noose around his neck. Left without management, their ship was at the mercy of wind and wave, with no living creature on deck save the big cat. He had vainly tried to break into the men's quarters, and failing in that, had laid siege to the cabin of the wireless operator. The door of this was fragile, however, and although the desperate man within had piled every article of furniture in the room against the door, there could be little doubt that it was but a matter of time when the maddened tiger would make use of his vast strength and burst in the frail barrier.

Such was the situation on board when, as a last resource, the devoted operator sent out the call for help that Bert had heard. The knowledge that help was at least on the way gave heart to the imprisoned and almost despairing man, and he waited for the rescuing ship to arrive with all the fortitude he could muster.

Meanwhile, on Bert's ship, Captain Manning had been summoned to the bridge, and had immediately ordered full steam ahead. The ship quivered and groaned as the steam rushed at high pressure into the cylinders, causing the great propellers to turn as though they had been but toys. Great clouds of black smoke poured from the funnel, and the ship forged ahead at a greater speed than her crew had ever supposed her capable of making.

Fast as was their progress, however, it seemed but a crawl to the anxious group gathered on the bridge, and Bert went below to send an encouraging message to the unfortunate operator on the other ship.

Crash! crash! and the powerful current crackled and flashed from the wires.

"Keep up courage," was the message Bert sent, "keep up courage, and we will get help to you soon. Are about ten knots from you now."

For a few minutes there was no reply, and, when the receiver finally clicked, Bert could hardly catch the answer, so faint was it.

"The dynamo has stopped," it read, "and batteries are almost exhausted. Heard shouting from the crew's quarters a short time ago, and think the tiger is probably trying to break in there. A—few minutes—more—" but here the sounder ceased, and Bert, in spite of his frantic efforts, was unable to get another word, good or bad. Finally, giving the attempt up as hopeless, he made his way to the bridge, where Captain Manning and the first officer were absorbed over a chart.

"We can't be very far from them now, sir," the latter was saying. "At the rate this old boat's going now we ought to sight them pretty soon, don't you think so, sir?"

"We surely should," replied the captain. "But I wonder if Wilson has heard any more from them. As long as—ah, here you are, eh, Mr. Wilson? What's the latest news from the distressed vessel?"

"Pretty bad, sir," said Bert. "The crew seems to have become panic-stricken, including the engine-room force, and they've allowed the dynamo to stop. The wireless man didn't have enough current left from the batteries to finish the message he was sending. He did say, though, that the tiger was raising a rumpus up forward, and trying to break into the men's quarters. I can only hope, sir, that we will not arrive too late."

"I hope so, indeed," responded Captain Manning, gloomily, "but even if we get there before the beast has gotten at them, we'll have our work cut out for us. We have no adequate weapons on board, and we can't hope to cope with a foe like that barehanded."

"That's very true," said the first officer, scratching his head. "I rather had a feeling that all we had to do was to get there and kill the tiger, but I must confess I hadn't figured out how. However," he added, "I've got a brace of pistols in my cabin, and I suppose you have, too, haven't you, sir?" addressing the captain.

"Oh, of course I have them," said the captain, impatiently, "but they're not much good in an affair of this kind. What we need is a big game rifle, and that's something we haven't got. However, I imagine we'll hit on some plan after we get there. Set your wits to work, Mr. Wilson, and see if you can't figure out a scheme. You have always struck me as being pretty ingenious."

"Well, I'll do my best, you may be sure of that, sir," replied Bert, "but meanwhile, I guess I'd better go below and see if by any chance they have got their wireless working again."

"Aye, aye," said the captain, "see what you can do, and I'll see that you are informed when we get near the vessel."

Bert did as he had proposed, but could get no response from his apparatus, and was just giving over the attempt as hopeless when he got a message from the captain that they were close up to the unfortunate ship.

Hastily unfastening the "harness" from his head, Bert rushed on deck, and gave a quick look about him. Sure enough, they were close aboard a rusty-looking steamer, that drifted aimlessly about, and at first glance seemed to have no living soul aboard. The deck was untenanted and showed no signs of life, and the silence was unbroken save for an occasional cry from the caged animals in the hold.

Of the tiger said to be loose on board there was no indication, however, but they soon made out a colored handkerchief waving from one of the portholes that afforded light and ventilation to the "fo'castle." Presently they heard someone shouting to them, but were unable to make out what was said.

Captain Manning ordered a boat lowered, and carefully picked the men whom he desired to go in it. When he had chosen almost his full crew, Bert hurried up to him, and said: "I beg your pardon, sir, but I would like to ask you a favor. Do you think you could allow me and my friend, Mr. Trent, to go along? I think we could do our share of what's to be done, and I feel that I ought to be among the party that goes in aid of a fellow operator."

At first the captain would not hear of any such proposition, but finally, by dint of much persuasion, Bert won a reluctant consent.

"All right," grumbled the captain. "If you must, you must, I suppose. But hurry up now. Step lively! All hands ready?"

"Aye, aye, sir," sang out the crew, and after a few parting instructions from Captain Manning, the first officer, Mr. Collins, shouted the order to give way.

The crew bent to their oars with a will, and the heavy boat fairly leaped through the water at their sturdy strokes. In almost less time than it takes to tell, the boat was under the porthole from which they had first seen the signals, and Mr. Collins was talking in a low voice with a white-faced man who peered out of the circular opening.

"He almost had us a little time back," said the latter, "but we managed to make enough noise to scare him away for the time. We haven't heard anything of him for quite a while now, but he's hungry, and he'll soon be back. Heaven help us, then, if you fellows can't do something for us."

"We'll get him, all right, never fear," said Mr. Collins, reassuringly, "but how do you stand now? How many did the beast get before you got away from him?"

"He killed the three animal keepers almost at one swipe," said the man, who proved to be the second mate. "Then the captain, as was a brave man, stood up to him with an old gun he used to keep in his cabin, and the beast crushed his head in before he could get the old thing to work. It must have missed fire, I guess. Then the brute started creeping toward us as was on deck, and we made a rush for the fo'castle door. The first officer happened to be the last one in, and the tiger just caught his arm with his claws and ripped it open to the bone. We managed to drag him in and slam the door in the beast's face, though, and then we piled everything we could lay hand to against the door."

"What did he do then?" inquired Mr. Collins.

"Why, he went ragin' back and made a dive for one of the stokers that was up at the engine-room hatchway gettin' a bit of fresh air, and he almost nabbed him. The dago dived below, though, and had sense enough to drop a grating after him. That stopped the cursed brute, and then I don't know what he did for a while. Just a little while ago, though, as I was tellin' ye, he came sniffin' and scratchin' around the door, and if he made a real hard try he'd get in, sure. Then it 'ud be good-night for us. Not one of us would get out of here alive."

"But now that he's left you for a time, why don't you make an attempt to trap or kill him?" inquired Mr. Collins, and there was a little contempt in his tone.

"What, us? Never in a hundred years," replied the man, in a scared voice. It was evident that the crew was completely unnerved, and Mr. Collins and his crew realized that if anything was to be done they must do it unaided.

"Well, here goes," said he. "We might as well get on that deck first as last. We'll never get anywhere by sitting here and talking." Accordingly, they clambered up on deck, one by one, led by the first mate. In a short time they were all safely on deck, and looked around, their hearts beating wildly, for any sign of the ferocious animal. As far as any evidences of his presence went, however, the nearest tiger might have been in Africa. There was a deathlike hush over the ship, broken at times by the muffled chattering of the monkeys confined in cages below decks.

All the men were armed with the best weapons they were able to obtain, consisting chiefly of heavy iron bars requisitioned from the engine-room.

Mr. Curtis, of course, had a pair of heavy revolvers, and both Bert and Dick had each a serviceable .45-calibre Colt. These were likely to prove of little avail against such an opponent, however, and more than one of the crew wished he were safely back on the deck of his own ship.

Not so Bert and Dick, however, and their eyes danced and sparkled from excitement. "Say," whispered Dick in Bert's ear, "talk about the adventures of that fellow you and I were reading about a day or two ago. This promises to outdo anything that I ever heard of."

"It sure does," said Bert, in the same suppressed voice. "I wonder where that beast can be hiding himself. This suspense is getting on my nerves."

All the rescuing party felt the same way, but the tiger obstinately refused to put in an appearance. The men started on an exploring expedition, beginning at the bow and working toward the stern. At every step they took, the probability of their presently stumbling on the animal became more imminent, and their nerves were keyed to the breaking point.

In this manner they traversed almost two-thirds of the deck, and were about to round the end of the long row of staterooms when suddenly, without a moment's warning, the tiger stood before them, not thirty feet away.

At first he seemed to be surprised, but as the men watched him, fascinated, they could see his cruel yellow eyes gradually change to black, and hear a low rumble issue from his throat. For a few seconds not one of them seemed able to move a hand, but then Mr. Curtis yelled, "Now's your time, boys. Empty your revolvers into him, Wilson and Crawford," and suiting the action to the word, he opened fire on the great cat.

Bert and Dick did likewise, but in their excitement most of their shots went wild, and only wounded the now thoroughly infuriated animal.

With a roar that fairly shook the ship the tiger leapt toward the hardy group. "Back! Back!" shouted Mr. Collins, and they retreated hastily. The tiger just fell short of them, but quickly gathered himself for another spring, and two of the more faint-hearted seamen started to run toward the bow. Indeed, it was a situation to daunt the heart of the bravest man, but Bert and the others who retained their self-control knew that it was now too late to retreat, and their only course, desperate as it seemed, was to stand their ground and subdue the raging beast if possible.

The tiger's rage was truly a terrible thing to see. As he stood facing them, foam dripped from his jaws, and great rumblings issued from his throat. His tail lashed back and forth viciously, and he began creeping along the deck toward them.

But now Bert and Dick and the first mate had had a chance, in frantic haste, to load their revolvers, and they gripped the butts of their weapons in a convulsive grasp. And they had need of all they could muster.

Soon the tiger judged he was near enough for a spring, and stopping, gathered his great muscles under him in tense knots. Then he sprang through the air like a bolt from a cross-bow, and this time they had no chance to retreat.

As the raging beast landed among them, the men scattered to left and right, and struck out with the heavy iron bars they had brought with them. They dodged this way and that, evading the tiger's ripping claws and snapping teeth as best they could, and landing a blow whenever the opportunity offered. They were not to escape unscathed from such an encounter, however, and again and again shouts of pain arose from those unable to avoid the raving beast. Bert and Dick waited until the tiger's attention was concentrated on three of the men who were making a concerted attack on him, and then, at almost point blank range, emptied their revolvers into the beast's head. At almost the same moment the first mate followed suit, and the tiger stopped in his struggles, and stood stupidly wagging his head from side to side, while bloody foam slavered and dripped from his jaws. Then he gradually slumped down on the reddened deck, and finally lay still, with once or twice a convulsive shiver running over him.

Quickly reloading their revolvers, Bert, Dick, and the first mate delivered another volley at the prostrate beast, so as to take no chances.

Every muscle in the animal's beautiful body relaxed, his great head rolled limply over on to the deck, and it was evident that he was dead. A cheer arose from the men, but their attention was quickly turned to themselves, and with good reason. Not one of them had escaped a more or less painful wound from the great beast's tearing claws, one or two of which threatened to become serious. Both Bert and Dick had deep, painful scratches about the arms and shoulders, but they felt glad enough to escape with only these souvenirs of the desperate encounter.

"Well, men," said Mr. Collins, after they had bound up their wounds temporarily, and were limping back toward their boat, "I think we can thank our lucky stars that we got off as easily as we did. When that fellow jumped for us the second time, I for one never expected to come out of the mix-up alive."

"I, either," said Bert. "I like excitement about as well as anybody, I guess, but this job of fighting tigers with nothing but a revolver is a little too rich for me. The next time I try it I'll want to pack a cannon along."

"Righto!" said Dick, with a laugh that was a trifle shaky. "But what are we going to do now? I suppose the first thing is to let those low-lives out of the forecastle and tell 'em we've fixed their tiger for them."

"We might as well," acquiesced Mr. Collins, and they lost no time in following out Dick's suggestion. Before they reached the forecastle they were joined by the two men who had run at the tiger's second onslaught, and you may be sure they looked thoroughly ashamed of themselves. The men who had stood fast realized that reproaches would do no good, however, and they were so exhilarated over their victory, now that they began to realize just what they had accomplished, that they were not inclined to indulge in recriminations. They could come later.

They were about to resume their march to the crew's quarters when Dick happened to notice that Bert was missing. The men all started out in search of him, but their anxiety was soon relieved by seeing Bert return accompanied by a man whom he presently introduced to them as the wireless operator. The latter was profuse in his expressions of gratitude, but Bert refused point blank to listen to him.

"It's no more than you would have done for us, if you had had the chance," he said, "therefore, thanks are entirely out of order."

"Not a bit of it," persisted the other, warmly. "It was a mighty fine thing for you fellows to do, and, believe me, I, for one, will never forget it."

By now they were in front of the fo'castle, and shouted out to the men within that they could come out with safety. There was a great noise of objects within being pulled away from the door, and then the crew of the animal ship emerged in a rather sheepish manner, for they realized that they had not played a very heroic part. However, they had had very little in the way of weapons, and perhaps their conduct might be palliated by this fact.

Two of them immediately set to work skinning the tiger, and meantime the wounded first mate of the animal ship expressed his thanks and that of the crew to Mr. Collins. Then the limping, smarting little band clambered over the side and into their waiting boat. The row back to the ship seemed to consume an age, but you may be sure that the two sailors who had escaped the conflict were now forced to do most of the hard work, and they did not even attempt to object, no doubt realizing the hopelessness of such a course.

They reached their ship at last, however, and were greeted with praise from the passengers on account of their bravery, and sympathy over their many and painful wounds.

After Mr. Collins had made his report to the captain, the latter shook his head gravely. "Perhaps I did wrong in letting you undertake such a task," he said, "but I don't know what else we could have done. Heaven knows how long it would have taken any other vessel to get here, and after they arrived they might not have had any greater facilities for meeting such a situation than we had. But I'm very glad we got out of the predicament without actual loss of life."

"We were very fortunate, indeed," agreed Mr. Collins, and here they dropped the subject, for among men who habitually followed a dangerous calling even such an adventure as this does not seem such a very unusual occurrence.

Bert was not so seriously wounded as to make it impossible to resume his duties, however, and after a few days his wounds gave him no further trouble. Needless to say, the remembrance of the desperate adventure never entirely left his mind to the end of his life, and for weeks afterward he would wake from a troubled sleep seeing again in his imagination the infuriated tiger as it had looked when leaping at the devoted group.

CHAPTER XII

AMONG THE CANNIBALS

The routine life of shipboard wore quietly on for several days without interruption. The staunch ship held steadily on its course, and the ceaseless vibrations of its engines came to be as unnoticed and as unthought of as the beatings of their own hearts. There had been no storms for some time, as indeed there seldom were at this time of the year, and Bert's duties as wireless operator occupied comparatively little of his time. He had plenty left, therefore, to spend with Dick and Tom, and they had little trouble in finding a way to occupy their leisure with pleasure and profit to themselves and others.

A favorite resort was the engine room, where in spite of the heat they spent many a pleasant hour in company with the chief engineer, MacGregor. The latter was a shaggy old Scotchman with a most stern and forbidding exterior, but a heart underneath that took a warm liking to the three comrades, much to the surprise and disgust of the force of stokers and "wipers" under him.

"And phwat do yez think of the old man?" one was heard to remark to his companion one day. "There was a toime when the chief 'ud look sour and grumble if the cap'n himself so much as poked his nose inside the engine room gratin', and now here he lets thim young spalpeens run all ovir the place, wid never a kick out o' him."

"Sure, an' Oi've ben noticin' the same," agreed his companion, "an' phwat's more, he answers all their questions wid good natur', and nivir seems to have ony desire to dhrop a wrinch on their noodles."

"Perhaps 'tis because the youngsters ask him nothin' but sinsible questions, as ye may have noticed," said he who had spoken first, as he leaned on his shovel for a brief rest. "Shure, an' it's me private opinion that the young cubs know 'most as much about the engines as old Mac himsilf."

"Thrue fer you," said the other. "Only yisterday, if O'im not mistaken, young Wilson, him as runs the wireless outfit for the ship, was down here, and they were havin' a argyment regardin' the advantages of the reciprocatin' engines over the new steam turbins, an' roast me in me own furnace if I don't think the youngster had the goods on the old man right up t' the finish."

"Oi wouldn't be su'prised at ahl, at ahl," agreed his companion. "The young felly has a head for engines, an' no mistake. He's got a lot o' book larnin' about 'em, too."

It was indeed as the stokers said, and a strong friendship and mutual regard had sprung up between the grizzled old engineer and the enthusiastic wireless operator. As our readers doubtless remember, Bert had been familiar with things mechanical since boyhood, and during his college course had kept up his knowledge by a careful reading of the latest magazines and periodicals given over to mechanical research. Needless to say, his ideas were all most modern, while on the part of the chief engineer there was a tendency to stick to the tried and tested things of mechanics and fight very shy of all inventions and innovations.

However, each realized that the other knew what he was talking about, and each had a respect for the opinions of the other. This did not prevent their having long arguments at times, however, in which a perfect shower and deluge of technical words and descriptions filled the air. It seldom happened, though, that either caused the other to alter his original stand in the slightest degree, as is generally the case in all arguments of any sort.

But the engineer was always ready to explain things about the ponderous engines that Bert did not fully understand, and there were constantproblems arising from Bert's inspection of the beautifully made machinery that only the engineer, of all on board, could solve for him. Bert always found a fascination in watching the powerful engines and would sit for hours at a time, when he was at leisure, watching each ingenious part do its work, with an interest that never flagged.

He loved to study the movements of the mighty pistons as they rose and fell like the arm of some immense giant, and speculate on the terrific power employed in every stroke. The shining, smooth, well-oiled machinery seemed more beautiful to Bert than any picture he had ever seen, and the regular click and chug of the valves was music. Every piece of brass, nickel and steel work in the engine room was spotlessly clean, and glittered and flickered in the glow from the electric lights.

Sometimes he and MacGregor would sit in companionable silence for an hour at a time, listening to the hiss of steam as it rushed into the huge cylinders, and was then expelled on the upward stroke of the piston. MacGregor loved his engines as he might a pet cat or dog, and often patted them lovingly when he was sure nobody was around to observe his actions.

Once the engineer had taken Bert back along the course of the big propeller shaft to where it left the ship, water being prevented from leaking in around the opening by means of stuffing boxes. At intervals the shaft was supported by bearings made of bronze, and as they passed them the old man always passed his hand over them to find out if by any chance one was getting warm on account of the friction caused by lack of proper lubrication.

"For it's an afu' thing," he said to Bert, shaking his head, "to have a shaft break when you're in the ragin' midst of a storm. It happened to me once, an' the second vayage I evir took as chief engineer, and I hae no desire t' repeat the experience."

"What did you do about it?" inquired Bert.

"We did the anly thing there was to be done, son. We set the whole engine room force drillin' holes thrae the big shaft, and then we riveted a wee snug collar on it, and proceeded on our way. Two days and two nights we were at it, with the puir bonnie ship driftin' helpless, an' the great waves nigh breakin' in her sides. Never a wink o' sleep did I get during the hale time, and none of the force under me got much more. Ye may believe it was a fair happy moment for all of us when we eased the steam into the low pressure cylinder and saw that the job was like to hold until we got tae port. Nae, nae, one experience like thot is sufficient tae hold a mon a lifetime."

"I should think it would be," said Bert. "You generally hear a lot about the romantic side of accidents at sea, but I guess the people actually mixed up in them look at the matter from a different point of view."

"Nae doot, nae doot," agreed the old Scotsman, "and what credit do ye suppose we got for all our work? The papers were full o' the bravery and cael headedness the skipper had exhibited, but what o' us poor deils wha' had sweated and slaved twae mortal day an nichts in a swelterin', suffercatin' hold, whi' sure death for us gin anything sprang a leak and the ship sank? Wae'd a' had nae chanct t' git on deck and in a boat. Wae'd have been drounded like wee rats in a trap. I prasume nobody thocht o' that, howiver."

"That's the way it generally works out, I've noticed," said Bert. "Of course, many times the captain does deserve much or all the credit, but the newspapers never take the trouble to find out the facts. You can bet your case wasn't the first of the kind that ever occurred."

"'Tis as you say," agreed the engineer; "but nae we must back to the engine room, me laddie. I canna feel easy when I am far frae it."

Accordingly they retraced their course, and were soon back in the room where the machinery toiled patiently day and night, never groaning or complaining when taken proper care of, as you may be sure these engines were. MacGregor would have preferred to have somebody make a slighting remark about him than about his idolized engines, and would have been less quick to resent it.

Bert was about to take his leave, when suddenly Tom and Dick came tumbling recklessly down the steep ladder leading to the engine room, and fairly fell down the last few rounds.

"Say, Bert, beat it up on deck," exclaimed Tom, as soon as he was able to get his breath. "We sighted an island an hour or so ago, and as we get nearer to it we can see that there's a signal of some sort on it. Captain Manning says that none of the islands hereabout are inhabited, so it looks as though somebody had been shipwrecked there. The skipper's ordered the course changed so as to head straight toward it, and we ought to be within landing distance in less than an hour."

"Hooray!" yelled Bert. "I'll give you a race up, fellows, and see who gets on deck first," and so saying he made a dive for the ladder. Dick and Tom made a rush to intercept him, but Bert beat them by a fraction of an inch, and went up the steep iron ladder with as much agility as any monkey. The others were close at his heels, however, and in less time than it takes to tell they were all on deck.

Dick and Tom pointed out the island to Bert, and there, sure enough, he saw what appeared to be a remnant of some flag nailed to an upright branch planted in the ground. They were not more than a mile from the island by this time, and soon Captain Manning rang the gong for half speed ahead. A few moments later he gave the signal to shut off power, and the vibration of the ship's engines ceased abruptly. The sudden stopping of the vibration to which by now they had become so accustomed that it seemed part of life came almost like a blow to the three young men, and they were obliged to laugh.

"Gee, but that certainly seems queer," said Tom. "It seems to me as though I must have been used to that jarring all my life."

"Well," said Dick, "it certainly feels unusual now, but I will be perfectly willing to exchange it for a little trip on good, solid land. I hope we can persuade the captain to let us go ashore with the men."

The captain's consent was easily obtained, and they then awaited impatiently for the boat to be launched that was to take them to the island.

The island was surrounded by a coral reef, in which at first there appeared to be no opening. On closer inspection, however, when they had rowed close up to it, they found a narrow entrance, that they would never have been able to use had the water been at all rough. Fortunately, however, the weather had been very calm for several days past, so they had little difficulty in manœuvering the boat through the narrow opening. As it was, however, once or twice they could hear the sharp coral projections scrape against the boat's sides, and they found time even in their impatience to land to wonder what would happen to any ship unfortunate enough to be tossed against the reef.

After they had passed the reef all was clear sailing, and a few moments later the boat grated gently on a sloping beach of dazzling white sand, and the sailor in the bow leapt ashore and drew the boat a little way up on the beach. Then they all jumped out and stood scanning what they could see of the place for some sign of life other than that of the signal they had seen from the ship. This now hung limply down around the pole, and no sound was to be heard save the lap of the waves against the reef and an occasional bird note from the rim of trees that began where the white sand ended.

The green trees and vegetation stood out in sharp relief contrasted with the white beach and the azure sky, and the three boys felt a tingle of excitement run through their veins. Here was just such a setting for adventures and romance as they had read about often in books, but had hardlydared ever hope to see. This might be an island where Captain Kidd had made his headquarters and buried priceless treasure, some of which at that moment might lie under the sand on which they were standing. The green jungle in front of them might contain any number of adventures and hair-raising exploits ready to the hand of any one who came to seek, and at the thought the spirits of all three kindled.

"This is the chance of a lifetime, fellows," said Bert, in a low voice, "if we don't get some excitement out of this worth remembering, I think it will be our own fault."

"That's what," agreed Dick, "why in time don't we get busy and do something. We won't find the person who put up that signal by standing here and talking. I want to make a break for those trees and see what we can find there."

"Same here," said Tom, "and I guess we're going to do something at last, by the looks of things."

Mr. Miller, the second mate, who had been placed in charge of the party, had indeed arrived at a decision, and now made it known to the whole group.

"I think the best thing we can do," he said, "is to skirt the forest there and see if we can find anything that looks like a path or trail. If there's any living thing on this island it must have left some sort of a trace."

This was done accordingly, and in a short time they were walking along the edge of the jungle, each one straining his eyes for any indication of a trail. At first they met with no success, but finally Tom gave a whoop. "Here we are," he yelled, "here's a path, or something that looks a whole lot like one, leading straight into the forest. Come along, fellows," and he started on a run along an almost obliterated trail that everybody else had overlooked.

You may be sure Bert and Dick were not far behind him, and were soon following close on his heels. After they had gone a short distance in this reckless fashion they were forced to slow down on account of the heat, which was overpowering. Also, as they advanced, the underbrush became thicker and thicker, and it soon became difficult to make any progress at all. Great roots and vines grew in tangled luxuriance across the path, and more than once one of them tripped and measured his length on the ground.

Soon they felt glad to be able to progress even at a walk, and Bert said, "We want to remember landmarks that we pass, fellows, so that we can be sure of finding our way back. It wouldn't be very hard to wander off this apology of a path, and find ourselves lost."

"Like the babes in the woods," supplemented Dick, with a laugh.

"Exactly," grinned Bert, "and I don't feel like doing any stunts along that line myself just at present."

These words were hardly out of his mouth when the path suddenly widened out into a little opening or glade, and the boys stopped abruptly to get their bearings.

"Look! over there, fellows," said Bert, in an excited voice. "If I'm not very much mistaken there's a hut over there, see, by that big tree—no, no, you simps, the big one with the wild grape vine twisted all over it. See it now?"

It was easy to see that they did, for they both hurried over toward the little shack at a run, but Bert had started even before they had, and beat them to it. They could gather little information from its contents when they arrived, however. Inside were a few ragged pieces of clothing, and in one corner a bed constructed of twigs and branches. In addition to these there was a rude chair constructed of boughs of trees, and tied together with bits of string and twine. It was evident from this, however, that some civilized person had at one time inhabited the place, and at a recent date, too, for otherwise the hut would have been in a more dilapidated condition than that in which they found it.

They rummaged around, scattering the materials of which the bed was constructed to left and right. Suddenly Tom gave a yell and pounced on something that he had unearthed.

"Why don't you do as I do, pick things up and look for them afterward?" he said, excitedly.

"What is it? What did you find?" queried Bert, who was more inclined to be sure of his ground before he became enthusiastic. "It looks a good deal like any other old memorandum book, as far as I can see."

"All right, then, we'll read it and see what is in it," replied Tom. "Why, it's a record of somebody's life on the island here. I suppose maybe you think that's nothing to find, huh?"

Without waiting for a reply he started to read the mildewed old book, and Bert and Dick read also, over his shoulder.

The first entry was dated about a month previous to the time of reading, and seemed to be simply a rough jotting down of the important events in the castaway's life for future reference. There were records of the man, whoever he might be, having found the spring beside which he had built the hut in which they were now standing; of his having erected the rude shelter, and a good many other details.

The three boys read the scribbled account with breathless interest, as Tom turned over page after page. "Come on, skip over to the last page," said Bert at last, "we can read all this some other time, and I'm crazy to know what happened to the fellow, whoever he is. Maybe he's written that down, too, since he seems to be so methodical."

In compliance with this suggestion, Tom turned to the last written page of the note-book, and what the boys read there caused them to gasp. It was scribbled in a manner that indicated furious haste, and read as follows:

"Whoever you are who read this, for heaven's sake come to my aid, if it is not too late. Last night I was awakened by having my throat grasped in a grip of iron, and before I could even start to struggle I was bound securely. By the light of torches held by my captors I could see that I was captured by a band of black-skinned savages. After securing me beyond any chance of escape, they paid little further attention to me, and held what was apparently a conference regarding my disposal. Finally they made preparations to depart, but first cooked a rude meal and my hands were unbound to enable me to eat. At the first opportunity I scrawled this account, in the hope that some party seeing my signal, might by chance find it, and be able to help me. As the savages travel I will try to leave some trace of our progress, so you can follow us. I only hope—" but here the message ended suddenly, leaving the boys to draw their own conclusions as to the rest of it.

For a few moments they gazed blankly into each other's faces, and uttered never a word. Bert was the first to break the silence.

"I guess it's up to us, fellows," he said, and the manly lines of his face hardened. "We've got to do something to help that poor devil, and the sooner we start the better. According to the dates in this book it must have been last Thursday night that he was captured, and this is Monday. If we hurry we may be able to trace him up and do something for him before it's too late."

The thought that they themselves might be captured or meet with a horrible death did not seem to enter the head of one of them. They simply saw plainly that it was, as Bert had said, "up to them" to do the best they could under the circumstances, and this they proceeded to do without further loss of time.

"The first thing to do," said Bert, "is to scout around and see if we can find the place where the savages left the clearing with their prisoner. Then it will be our own fault if we cannot follow the trail."

This seemed more easily said than done, however, and it was some time before the three, fretting and impatient at the delay, were able to find any clue. At last Bert gave an exultant whoop and beckoned the others over to where he stood.

"I'll bet any amount of money this is where they entered the jungle," he said, exultantly. "Their prisoner evidently evaded their observation while they were breaking a path through, and pinned this on the bush here," and he held up a corner of a white linen handkerchief, with the initial M embroidered on the corner.

"Gee, I guess you're right," agreed Dick. "Things like that don't usually grow on bushes. It ought to be easy for us to trace the party now."

This proved to be far from the actual case, however, and if it had not been for the occasional scraps of clothing fluttering from a twig or bush every now and then their search would have probably ended in failure. So rank and luxuriant is the jungle growth in tropical climates, that although in all probability a considerable body of men had passed that way only a few days before, practically all trace of their progress was gone. The thick underbrush grew as densely as ever, and it would have seemed to one not skilled in woodland arts that the foot of man had never trod there. Monkeys chattered in the trees as they went along, and parrots with rainbow plumage shot among the lofty branches, uttering raucous cries. Humming clouds of mosquitoes rose and gathered about their heads, and added to the heat to make their journey one of torment.

Their previous experience as campers now stood them in good stead, and they read without much trouble signs of the progress of the party in front of them that they must surely have missed otherwise.

After three hours of dogged plodding, in which few words were exchanged, Bert said, "I don't think we can have very much further to go, fellows. I remember the captain saying that this island was not more than a few miles across in any direction, and we must have traveled some distance already. We're bound to stumble on their camp soon, so we'd better be prepared."

"Probably by this time," said Tom, "the savages will have returned to the mainland, or some other island from which they came. I don't think it very likely that they live permanently on this one. It seems too small."

"Yes, I thought of that," said Bert, "but we've got to take our chance on that. If they are gone, there is nothing else we can do, and we can say we did our best, anyway."

"But what shall we do when we find them?" asked Tom, after a short pause, "provided, of course, that our birds haven't flown."

"Oh, we'll have to see how matters stand, and make our plans accordingly," replied Bert. "You fellows had better make sure your revolvers are in perfect order. I have a hunch that we'll need them before we get through with this business."

Fortunately, before leaving the ship the boys had, at Bert's suggestion, strapped on their revolvers, and each had slipped a handful of cartridges into their pockets.

"The chances are a hundred to one we won't need them at all," Bert had said at the time. "But if anything should come up where we'll need them, we'll probably be mighty glad we brought them."

The boys were very thankful for this now, as without the trusty little weapons their adventure would have been sheer madness. As it was, however, the feel of the compact .45's was very reassuring, and they felt that they would at least have a fighting chance, if worse came to worst, and they were forced to battle for their lives.

CHAPTER XIII

THE HUNTING WOLVES

They advanced more cautiously now, with every sense alert to detect the first sign of any lurking savage. They had not proceeded far in this manner when Bert, who was slightly in the lead, motioned with his hand in back of him for them to stop. This they did, almost holding their breath the while, trying to make out what Bert had seen or heard. For several seconds he stood the very picture of attention and concentration, and then turned to them.

"What is it, Bert, do you see anything?" inquired Dick, in a subdued but tense whisper.

"Not a thing as yet," answered Bert, in the same tone, "but I thought I smelled smoke, and if I did, there must be a camp-fire of some kind not very far away. Don't you fellows smell it?"

Both sniffed the air, and as a slight breeze suddenly blew against their faces, Tom said, "Gee, Bert, I smell it now!"

"So do I!" said Dick, almost at the same instant, and the hearts of all three began to beat hard. They had evidently trailed the party of savages to their camp, and now they had something of the feeling of the lion hunter who suddenly comes unexpectedly upon his quarry and is not quite certain what to do with it when cornered. Needless to say, they had never faced any situation like this before, and it is not to be wondered at if they felt a little nervous over attempting to take a prisoner out from the midst of a savage camp, not even knowing what might be the force or numbers of the enemy they would have to cope with.

This feeling was but momentary, however, and almost immediately gave place to a fierce excitement and a wild exultation at the prospect of danger and conflict against odds. Each knew the others to be true and staunch to their heart's core, and as much to be relied on as himself. They felt sure that at least they were capable of doing as much or more than anybody else under the circumstances, and so the blood pounded through their veins and their eyes sparkled and danced as they drew together to hold a "council of war."

There was little to be discussed, however, as they all three felt that the only thing to do was to "face the music and see the thing through to the finish," as Bert put it.

Accordingly they shook hands, and drew their revolvers, so as to be ready for any emergency at a moment's notice. Then, with Bert once more in the lead, they took up their interrupted march. For all the noise they made, they might have been the savages themselves. Their early training in camp and field now proved invaluable, and not a twig cracked or a leaf rustled at their cautious approach. Soon a patch of light in front of them indicated a break in the jungle, and they crouched double as they advanced. Suddenly Bert made a quick motion with his hand, and darted like a streak into the underbrush at the side of the trail. The others did likewise, and not a moment too soon. A crackling of the undergrowth cluttering the path announced the approach of a considerable body of men, and in a few moments the boys, from their place of concealment, where they could look out from the leafy underbrush with little chance of being seen, saw a party of eight or ten dusky warriors pass by, apparently bent on foraging, for each carried a large bag slung over his shoulder.

They were big, splendidly built men, but their faces indicated a very low order of intelligence. Their features were large, coarse, and brutish, and the boys were conscious of a shudder passing over them as they thought of being at the mercy of such creatures.

The savages seemed in a good humor just then, however, for every once in a while they laughed among themselves, evidently at something humorous one of them was reciting. It was well for our heroes that they were so, for otherwise they could hardly have failed to notice signs of their recent presence on the trail. Fortunately this did not happen, however, and soon they were swallowed up in the dense jungle.

Shortly afterward the boys emerged from their places of concealment, and resumed their slow advance. They were soon at the edge of the clearing, and then halted to reconnoitre before venturing further.

The savages were encamped in a natural hollow, and had apparently made arrangements for quite a protracted visit. They had constructed rude huts or lean-tos of branches and leaves, scattered at any place that seemed convenient. Naked children shouted noisily as they played and rolled on the green turf, and made such a noise that the parrots in the woods were frightened, and flew away with disgusted squawks.

In the center of the encampment were two huts evidently constructed with more care than the others, and around both were squatted sentries with javelins lying on the ground within easy reach.

"I'll bet any money they are keeping their prisoner in one of those shacks, fellows," said Bert, "but what do you suppose the other one is for? It looks bigger than the others."

"Oh, that's probably the king's palace," said Dick. "Compared to the rest of those hovels it almost looks like one, at that."

"That's what it is, all right," agreed Tom, "but how are we going to tell which one is the prisoner's, and which the king's? We don't want to go and rescue the wrong one, you know."

"No danger of that," said Bert. "All we've got to do is to lie low a little while and see what's going on down there. We'll find out how matters stand soon enough."

Accordingly, the trio concealed themselves as best they could, and in whispers took council on the best means of bringing about the release of the captive.

This proved a knotty problem, however, and for a long while they seemed no nearer its solution. It was Bert who finally proposed the plan that they eventually followed.

"I think," he said, "that we'd better get the lay of the land securely in our eye, and then wait till dark and make our attempt. We haven't got any chance otherwise, as far as I can see. It would be nonsense to rush them in the broad light of day, for we'd simply be killed or captured ourselves, and that wouldn't improve matters much. There will be a full moon, almost, to-night, and this clearing isn't so big but what we might be able to sneak from the shadow of the trees up close to the two center huts. Then we could overpower the sentries, if we have luck, and smuggle the prisoner into the woods. Once there, we'll have to take our chance of keeping them off with our revolvers, if they pursue and overtake us. Can either of you think of a better plan than that?"

It seemed that neither could, and so they resolved to carry out Bert's. Accordingly, they kept their positions till the sun gradually sank, and the shadows began to creep over the little clearing. The night descended very quickly, however, as it always does in tropical latitudes, but it seemed an age to the impatient boys before the jungle was finally enshrouded in inky shadows, and it became time for them to make their desperate attempt. Stealthy rustlings and noises occasionally approached them as they lay, and more than once they thought their hiding-place had been discovered. At last, Bert decided that the time had come to put their plan into action, and they rose stealthily from their cramped position. The prospect of immediate action was like a strong stimulant to these three tried comrades, and all thought of danger and possible, nay, even probable, death, or what might be infinitely worse, capture, was banished from their minds. They had often craved adventure, and now they seemed in a fair way to get their fill of it.

Quietly as cats they stole around the edge of the clearing, planting each footstep with infinite care to avoid any possible sound. Once a loud shouting arose from the camp, and they made sure that they were discovered, and grasped their revolvers tightly, resolved to sell their lives dearly. It proved to be merely some disturbance among the savages, however, and they ventured to breathe again.

Foot by foot they skirted the clearing, guided by the fitful and flickering light of the camp-fire, and finally gained a position in what they judged was about the rear of the two central huts.

Now there was nothing to do but wait until the majority of the camp should fall asleep, and this proved the most trying ordeal they had yet experienced. At first groups of boisterous children approached their place of concealment, and more than once their hearts leapt into their mouths as it seemed inevitable that they would be discovered by them. As luck would have it, however, the children decided to return to the fire, and so they escaped at least one peril.

Gradually the noises of the camp diminished, and the fire flickered and burnt low. It was now the turn of the jungle insects, and they struck up a chorus that seemed deafening. Also, the mosquitoes issued forth in swarms, and drove the three boys almost frantic, for they did not dare to change their positions or make any effort to ward off the humming pests, as the noise entailed in doing so would have been almost certain to betray them.

There is an end to the longest wait, however, and at Bert's low whisper they crept toward the two huts they had marked in the center of the village. The moon was not yet high over the trees, and threw thick patches of inky blackness, that served our three adventurers well.

At times they could hardly make out each other's forms, so deep were the shadows, and they breathed a prayer of thankfulness for this aid.

The shadows fell at least ten feet short of the huts, however, and across this open space it was evident they would have to dash and take their chances of being seen.

As they had watched from the woods earlier in the evening, they had seen that the guard around the huts consisted of two men for each. The huts were perhaps forty feet apart, and this made it possible for them to attack the sentries guarding the one in which the prisoner was confined without necessarily giving the alarm to those about the other shack.

The boys were near enough to the dusky sentries now to hear their voices as they exchanged an occasional guttural remark. Bert touched the other two lightly, and they stopped. "I'll take the fellow nearest the fire," he breathed, "you two land on the other one. Club him with your revolvers, but whatever you do, don't let him make a sound, or we're gone for sure. Understand?"

"Sure," they whispered, and all prepared to do their parts. At a whispered word from Bert, they dashed with lightning speed across the patch of moonlight, and before the astonished sentries could utter a cry were upon them like so many whirlwinds. Bert grasped the man he had selected by the throat, and dealt him a stunning blow on the head with the butt of his revolver. The blow would have crushed the skull of any white man, but it seemed hardly to stun the thickheaded savage. He wriggled and squirmed, and Bert felt his arm go back toward the sash round his waist, feeling for the wicked knife that these savages always wore.

Bert dared not let go of his opponent's throat, as he knew that one cry would probably ring their death knell. He retained his grasp on his enemy's windpipe, therefore, but dropped his revolver and grasped the fellow's wrist. They wrestled and swayed, writhing this way and that, but fortunately the soft moss and turf under them deadened the sound of their struggles.

Bert had met his match that night, however, and, strain as he might, he felt his opponent's hand creeping nearer and nearer the deadly knife. He realized that his strength could not long withstand the terrific strain put upon it, and he resolved to make one last effort to beat the savage at his own game. Releasing the fellow's sinewy wrist, he made a lightning-like grasp for the hilt of the knife, and his fingers closed over it a fraction of a second ahead of those of the black man. Eluding the latter's frantic grasp at his wrist, he plunged the keen and heavy knife into the shoulder of his opponent. Something thick and warm gushed over his hand, and he felt the muscles of his enemy go weak. Whether dead or unconscious only, he was for the time being harmless. Bert himself was so exhausted that for a few moments he lay stretched at full length on the earth, unable to move or think.

In a few moments his strong vitality asserted itself, however, and he gathered strength enough to go to the assistance of his comrades. It was not needed, though, for they had already choked the remaining guard into unconsciousness.

They waited a few moments breathlessly, to see if the noise, little as it had been, had aroused the rest of the camp. Apparently it had not, and they resolved to enter the hut without further loss of time.

This was accomplished with little difficulty, and they were soon standing in the interior of the shack, which was black as any cave. The boys had feared that there would be another guard in the place, who might give the alarm before he could be overpowered, but they now saw that this fear had been groundless.

A torch, stuck in a chink in the wall, smoked and flared, and by its uncertain light they could make out the form of a man bound securely to one of the corner posts. He gazed at them without saying a word, and seemed unable to believe the evidence of his senses.

"What—what—how—" he stammered, but Bert cut him short.

"Never mind talking now, old man," he said. "It's a long story, and we'd better not wait to talk now. We're here, but it remains to be seen if we ever get away, or become candidates for a cannibal feast ourselves."

"How did you get past the sentries?" asked the prisoner.

"Well, we didn't wait to get their consent, you can bet on that," returned Bert, "and I don't think, now that we are here, that they'll offer any objections to our leaving, either. But now, it's up to us to get you untied, and make a quick sneak. Somebody's liable to come snooping around here almost any time, I suppose."

"You may be sure we can't leave any too soon to suit me," said the captive. "I believe, from all that I have been able to gather from their actions, that I was to furnish the material for a meal for the tribe to-morrow. They're head hunters and cannibals, and the more space I put between them and me the better I shall be pleased."

While he had been speaking, the boys had been busily engaged in cutting the cords that bound him, and now they assisted him to his feet. He had been bound in one position so long, however, that he could hardly stand at first, and Bert began to fear that he would not be able to move. After a few moments, however, his powers began to come back to him, and in a few minutes he seemed able to walk.

"All right, fellows, I guess we won't wait to pay our respects to the king," said Bert. "Let's get started. Do you feel able to make a dash now?" he inquired, addressing the erstwhile prisoner.

The latter signified that he was, and they prepared to leave without further discussion. When they got outside, they found that they were favored by a great piece of good fortune. The moon was now in such a position that it threw the shadow of a particularly tall tree almost to the hut, and they quickly made for the welcome security it offered. They made as little noise as possible, but their companion was less expert in the ways of the woods than they, and more than once slipped and fell, making a disturbance that the boys felt sure would be heard by someone in the camp.

Fate was kind to them, however, and at last they reached the shelter of the woods without apparently having given the savages any cause for suspicion. Once well in the jungle, they felt justified in making more speed without bothering so much about the noise. After a little trouble they found the trail that they had followed to the camp, and started back toward the coast with the best speed they could muster.

In the dense shadows cast by the arching trees they could hardly see a foot ahead of them, and continually stumbled, tripped, and fell over the roots and creepers in their path.

Their progress became like a horrible nightmare, in which one is unable to make any headway in fleeing from a pursuing danger, no matter how hard one tries. They were haunted by the fear of hearing the yell of the savages in pursuit, for they knew that if they were overtaken, here in the narrow path, in pitch darkness, they would be slaughtered by an unseen enemy without the chance to fight. The experienced savages could come at them from all sides through the forest, and have them at a terrible disadvantage.

"If we can only make that rocky little hill we passed coming to this infernal place, fellows," panted Bert, "we can stay there till daylight, and at least make a fight for our lives. If they should catch us here now, they could butcher us like rats in a trap."

In compliance with these words, they made desperate efforts to hurry their pace, and were beginning to pluck up hope. Suddenly their hearts stood still, and then began to beat furiously.

Far behind them in the mysterious, deadly jungle, they heard a weird, eerie shrill cry.

"What was it? What was it?" whispered Tom, in a low, horror-struck voice.

The man whom they had freed made one or two efforts to speak, but his words refused to come at first. Then he said, in a dry, hard voice, "I know what it is. That was the cry their hunting wolves give when they are on the trail of their quarry. May heaven help us now, for we are dead men."

"Hunting wolves?" said Bert, in a strained voice, "what do you mean?"

"They're three big wolves the savages captured at some time, and they have trained them to help run down game in the hunt, the same as we have trained dogs. Only these brutes are far worse than any dog, and a thousand times more savage. If they get us—" but here his voice trailed down into silence, for again they heard that fierce cry, but this time much nearer.

The little party broke into a desperate run, and blundered blindly, frantically forward. The mysterious, danger-breathing jungle surrounding them on every side, the horrible pursuit closing in on them from behind, caused their hair to rise with an awful terror that lent wings to their feet. They stumbled, fell, picked themselves and each other up again, and hastened madly forward in their wild race.

"If we can only make it, if we can only make it," Bert repeated over and over to himself, while the breath came in great sobbing gasps from between his lips. He was thinking of their one last chance of safety—the little knoll that he had marked as they followed the savages' trail the previous day as a possible retreat if they were pursued.

Loud and weird came the baying of the beasts on their trail, but Bert, straining his eyes ahead, could make out a little patch of moonlight through the trees.

"Faster, fellows, faster," he gasped. "A little further, and we'll be there. Faster, faster!"

With a last despairing effort they dashed into the clearing, which was flooded with silvery moonlight. Now, at least, they would be able to see and fight, and their natural courage came back to them.

"Get up on that big rock in the center!" yelled Bert, "for your lives, do you hear me? for your lives!"

They scrambled madly up the huge boulder, Bert helping them and being pulled up last by Dick and Tom. Dropping on the flat top of the rock, perhaps seven or eight feet from the ground, they drew their revolvers and faced toward the opening in the trees from which they had dashed a few moments before.

Nor had they long to wait. From the jungle rushed three huge wolves, forming such a spectacle as none of the little party ever forgot to his dying day. The hair bristled on their necks and backs, and foam dropped from their jaws. As they broke from the line of trees they gave utterance once more to their blood-curdling bay, but then caught sight of the men grouped on the big boulder, and in terrible silence made straight for them.

Without stopping they made a leap up the steep sides of the rock. Almost at the same instant the three revolvers barked viciously, and one big brute dropped back, biting horribly at his ribs, and then running around the little glade in circles. The other two scrambled madly at the rock, trying to get a foothold, and one grasped Dick's shoe in his teeth. A second later, however, and before his jaws even had a chance to close, the three guns spoke at once, and the animal dropped quivering back upon the ground. The third beast seemed somewhat daunted by the fate of his comrades, and was moreover wounded slightly himself. He dropped back and took up a position about ten feet from the boys' place of refuge, and throwing back his head, gave utterance to a dismal howl. Faintly, as though answering him, the boys heard a yell, that they knew could be caused by none but the savages themselves.

It seemed hopeless to fight against such odds, but these young fellows were not made of the stuff that gives up easily. Where the spirit of others might have sunk under such repeated trials, theirs only became more stubborn and more determined to overcome the heavy odds fate had meted out to them.

Taking careful aim Bert fired at the remaining wolf, and his bullet fulfilled its mission. The brute dropped without a quiver, and Bert slid to the ground.

"Come on, fellows," he yelled, "get busy here and help me build a fort. We've got to roll some of these rocks into position in a little less than no time, so we can give them an argument when they arrive."

"Oh, what's the use?" said the man whom they had rescued, in a hopeless voice. "We haven't got any chance against them. We might as well surrender first as last, and take our chances of escaping afterward."

"Why, man, what are you talking about?" said Dick, scornfully. "You don't think we're going to give in without a struggle, do you, when we have some shelter here and guns in our hands? Not on your life, we won't, and don't you forget it."

"Well, I was just giving you my opinion, that's all," said the man, who, it must be confessed, spoke in a rather shamefaced manner. "We're sure to be butchered if we follow out your plan, though, mark my words."

"Well, we'll at least send some of them to their last accounting before they do get to us," said Bert. "Step lively, now, and help us, instead of talking in that fool way."

While this talk had been going on the boys had rolled several big boulders up against the one that had already offered them such timely aid, in such a manner as to form a little enclosed space or fort. In their excitement and pressing need they accomplished feats of strength that under ordinary circumstances they would not even have attempted or believed possible.

Soon they had made every preparation they could think of, and with set teeth and a resolve to fight to the last gasp waited the coming of the pursuing cannibals.

Soon they could hear them rushing through the forest, exchanging deep-throated cries, and a few moments later they burst into the clearing. When they saw the preparations that had been made for their reception, however, they paused, and some pointed excitedly toward the three dead wolves. It was evident that they had been more prepared to see the mangled bodies of their erstwhile prisoner and his rescuers, rather than what they actually did find.

Bert, seeing that they were disconcerted, decided to open hostilities. With a wild yell, he started firing his revolver toward the closely-grouped savages, taking careful aim with each shot. A much poorer shot than Bert would have had difficulty in missing such a mark, and every bullet took deadly effect.

All at once panic seemed to seize on the savages, and they rushed madly back into the jungle. Of course, Bert wasted no more valuable ammunition firing at an unseen enemy, and a breathless hush fell over the scene.

At first the little party expected the savages to renew the conflict, but the time wore slowly on and nothing of the kind happened. They kept a keen lookout to guard against a surprise, but none was attempted.

At length dawn broke, and the sun had never been so welcome to the boys as it was then. In the light of day their experience seemed like an awful dream, or would have seemed so, had it not been for the bodies of the three wolves.

The besieged party held a "pow-wow," and as it was clear that they could not stay where they were indefinitely, they decided to make a break for the ship without further delay.

After a careful reconnoitering of the path, they ventured into it with many misgivings, but could see no sign of the head hunters. They made the best possible speed, and it was not very long before they reached the beach.

Needless to say, the whole ship's company had been greatly worried over their absence, but their relief was correspondingly great at their safe return. The captain had reinforced Mr. Miller's complement of men with orders to go in search of the three boys as soon as morning broke. He was prepared to hold them strictly to account for what he thought their rashness, but repressed his censure when he heard their story. The boat was swung inboard, the Fearless gathered way, and the island receding to a point was soon lost to sight in the distance.

CHAPTER XIV

THE LAND OF SURPRISES

"Better fifty years of EuropeThan a cycle of Cathay,"

murmured Dick, yielding once more to his chronic habit of quotation.

They had reached the gateway of Southern China and cast anchor in the harbor of Hong-Kong. It had been a day of great bustle and confusion, and all hands had been kept busy from the time the anchor chain rattled in the hawse-hole until dusk began to creep over the waters of the bay. The great cranes had groaned with their loads as they swung up the bales and boxes from the hold and transferred them to the lighters that swarmed about the sides of the Fearless. The passengers, eager once more to be on terra firma after the long voyage, had gone ashore, and the boat was left to the officers and crew. These had been kept on board by the manifold duties pertaining to their position, but were eagerly looking forward to the morrow, when the coveted shore leave would be granted in relays to the crew, while the officers would be free to go and come almost as they pleased. It was figured that even with the greatest expedition in discharging cargo and taking on the return shipments for the "States," it would be nearly or quite a week before they began their return journey, and they promised themselves in that interval to make the most of their stay in this capital of the Oriental commercial world.

Now, as dusk fell over the waters, the boys sat at the rail and gazed eagerly at the strange sights that surrounded them. The harbor was full of shipping gathered from the four quarters of the world. On every side great liners lay, ablaze with light from every cabin and porthole. Native junks darted about saucily here and there, while queer yellow faces looked up at them from behind the mats and lateen-rigged sails. The unforgettable smells of an Eastern harbor assailed their nostrils. The high pitched nasal chatter of the boatmen wrangling or jesting, was unlike anything they had ever before heard or imagined. Everything was so radically different from all their previous experiences that it seemed as though they must have kneeled on the magic carpet of Solomon and been transported bodily to a new world.

Before them lay the city itself glowing with myriad lights. The British concession with its splendid buildings, its immense official residences, its broad boulevards, might have been a typical European city set down in these strange Oriental surroundings. But around and beyond this lay the real China, almost as much untouched and uninfluenced by these modern developments as it had been for centuries. Great hills surrounded the city on every side, and temples and pagodas uprearing their quaint sloping roofs indicated the location of the original native quarters. In the distance they could see the lights of the little cable railway that carried passengers to the heights from which they could obtain a magnificent view of the harbor and the surrounding country.

The ship's doctor had come up just as Dick had finished his quotation.

"Yes," he assented, as he lit a fresh cigar and drew his chair into the center of the group. "The poet might have gone further than that and intimated that even one year of Europe would be better than a 'cycle of Cathay.' There's more progress ordinarily in a single year among Europeans than there is here in twenty centuries."

They gladly made room for him. The doctor was a general favorite and a cosmopolitan in all that that word implies. He seemed to have been everywhere and seen everything. In the course of his profession he had been all over the world, and knew it in every nook and corner. He had a wealth of interesting experiences, and had the gift of telling them, when in congenial company, in so vivid and graphic a way, that it made the hearer feel as though he himself had taken part in the events narrated.

"Of course," went on the doctor, "it all depends on the point of view. If progress is a good thing, we have the advantage of the Chinese. If it is a bad thing, they have the advantage of us. Now, they say it is a bad thing. With them 'whatever is is right.' Tradition is everything. What was good enough for their parents is good enough for them. They live entirely in the past. They cultivate the ground in the same way and with the same implements that their fathers did two thousand years ago. To change is to offend the gods. All modern inventions are devices of the devil. Every event in their whole existence is governed by cut and dried rules. From the moment of birth to that of death, life moves along one fixed groove. They don't want railroads or telephones or phonographs or machinery or anything else that to us seems a necessity of life. Whatever they have of these has been forced upon them by foreigners. A little while ago they bought up a small railroad that the French had built, paid a big advance on the original price, and then threw rails and locomotives into the sea."

"Even our 'high finance' railroad wreckers in Wall Street wouldn't go quite as far as that," laughed Tom.

"No," smiled the doctor, "they'd do it just as effectively, but in a different way."

"And yet," interposed Dick, "the Chinese don't seem to me to be a stupid race. We had one or two in our College and they were just as bright as anyone there."

"They're not stupid by any means," replied the doctor. "There was a time, thousands of years ago, when they were the very leaders of civilization. They had their inventors and their experimenters. Why, they found out all about gunpowder and printing and the mariner's compass, when Europe was sunk in the lowest depths of ignorance. At that time, the intellect of the people was active and productive. But then they seem to have had a stroke of paralysis, and they've never gotten over it."

"It always seemed to me," said Bert, "that 'Alice in Wonderland' should really have been called 'Alice in China-land.' She and her mad hatter and the March hare and the Cheshire cat would certainly have felt at home here."

"True enough," rejoined the doctor. "It isn't without reason that this has been called 'Topsy-turvy' land."

"For instance," he went on, "you could never get into a Chinaman's head what Shakespeare meant when he said: 'A rose by any other name would smell as sweet.' The roses in China have no fragrance.

"Take some other illustrations. When we give a banquet, the guest of honor is seated at the right of the host as a special mark of distinction. In China, he is placed at the left. If you meet a friend in the street, out goes your hand in greeting. The Chinaman shakes hands with himself. If an American or European is perplexed about anything he scratches his head. When the Chinaman is puzzled, he scratches his foot."

The comicality of this idea was too much for the gravity of the boys—never very hard to upset at any time—and they roared with laughter. Their laugh was echoed more moderately by Captain Manning, who, relieved at last of the many duties attendant upon the first day in port, had come up behind them and now joined the group. The necessity of keeping up the strain and dignity of his official position had largely disappeared with the casting of the anchor, and it was more with the easy democracy and good fellowship of the ordinary passenger that he joined in the conversation.

"They have another queer custom in China that bears right on the doctor's profession," he said, with a sly twinkle in his eye. "Here they employ a doctor by the year, but they only pay him as long as the employer keeps well. The minute he gets sick, the doctor's salary ceases, and he has to work like sixty to get him well in a hurry, so that his pay may be resumed."

"Well," retorted the doctor, "I don't know but they have the better of us there. It is certainly an incentive to get the patient well at once, instead of spinning out the case for the sake of a bigger fee. I know a lot of fashionable doctors whose income would go down amazingly if that system were introduced in America."

"You'll find, too," said the captain, "that the Chinaman's idea of what is good to eat is almost as different from ours as their other conceptions. There's just about one thing in which they agree with us, and that is on the question of pork. They are very fond of this, and you have all read, no doubt, the story told by Charles Lamb of the Chinese peasant whose cabin was burned, together with a pig who had shared it with the family. His despair at the loss of the pig was soon turned to rejoicing when he smelled the savory odor of roast pork and learned for the first time how good it was. But, outside of that, we don't have much in common. They care very little for beef or mutton. To make up for this, however, they have made a good many discoveries in the culinary line that they regard as delicacies, but that you won't find in any American cook book. Rats and mice and edible birds' nests and shark fins are served in a great variety of ways, and those foreigners who have had the courage to wade through the whole Chinese bill of fare say it is surprising to find out how good it is. After all, you can get used to anything, and we Europeans and Americans are becoming broader in our tastes than we used to be. Horse meat is almost as common as beef in Berlin; dogs are not disdained in some parts of France, and only the other day I read of a banquet in Paris where they served stuffed angleworms and pronounced them good."

"I imagine it will be a good while, however, before we get to the point where rats and mice are served in our restaurants," said Tom, with a grimace.

"Yes," rejoined the captain, "we'll probably draw the line there and never step over it. But you'll have a chance pretty soon to sample Chinese cooking, and if you ask no questions and eat what is set before you, you will probably find it surprisingly good. 'What the eye doesn't see the heart doesn't grieve over,' you know. And when you come to the desserts, you will find that there are no finer sweetmeats in the world than those served at Chinese tables."

"Another thing that seems queer to us Western people," said the doctor, "is their idea of the seat of intellect. We regard it as the head. They place it in the stomach. If the Chinaman gets off what he thinks to be a witty thing, he pats his stomach in approval."

"I suppose when his head is cut off, he still goes on thinking," grinned Tom.

"That wouldn't phase a Chinaman for a minute," answered the doctor. "He'd retort by asking you if you'd go on thinking if they cut you in half."

"Then, if you wanted to praise a Chinese author, I suppose, instead of alluding to his 'bulging brow,' it would be good form to refer to his 'bulging stomach,'" laughed Ralph.

"Gee," put in Tom, "if that were so, I've seen some fat people in the side shows at the circus that would have it all over Socrates."

"There's one thing," went on the doctor, "where they set us an example that we well might follow, and that is in the tolerance they have for the religious views of other people. There isn't any such thing as persecution or ostracism in China on the score of religious belief. There are three or four religions and all are viewed with approval and kindly toleration. A man, for instance, will meet several strangers in the course of business or of travel, and they will fall into conversation. It is etiquette to ask the religious belief of your new acquaintances, so our Chinaman asks the first of them: 'Of what religion are you?' 'I practice the maxims of Confucius,' is the response. 'Very good, and you?' turning to the second. 'I am a follower of Lao-tze.' The third answers that he is a Buddhist, and the first speaker winds up the conversation on this point by shaking hands—with himself— and genially remarking: 'Ah, well, we are all brothers after all.'"

"They certainly have the edge on us there," remarked Bert. "I wish we had a little of that spirit in our own country. We could stand a lot more of it than we have."

"Outside of the question of religion, however," went on the doctor, "we might think that they carry politeness too far to suit our mode of thinking. If you should meet a friend and ask after the health of his family, you would be expected to say something like this: 'And how is your brilliant and distinguished son, the light of your eyes and future hope of your house, getting on?' To this your friend would probably reply: 'That low blackguard and detestable dog that for my sorrow is called my son is in good health, but does not deserve that your glorious highness should deign to ask about him.'"

"You will notice," said the captain when the laugh had subsided, "that the doctor uses the son as an illustration. The poor daughter wouldn't even be inquired about. She is regarded as her father's secret sorrow, inflicted upon him by a malignant decree of fate. In a commercial sense, the boy is an asset; the girl is a liability. You hear it said sometimes, with more or less conviction, that the world we live in is a 'man's world.' However that may be modified or denied elsewhere, it is the absolute truth as regards China. If the scale of a nation's civilization is measured by the way it treats its women, — and I believe this to be true, — then the Celestial Kingdom ranks among the very lowest. From the time she comes, unwelcomed, into the world, until, unmourned, she leaves it, her life is not worth living. She is the slave of the household, and, in the field, she pulls the plough while the man holds the handles. In marriage, she is disposed of without the slightest reference to her own wishes, but wholly at the whim of her parents, and often sees the bridegroom's face for the first time when he comes to take her to his own house. There she is as much a slave as before. Her husband can divorce her for the most flimsy reasons and she has no redress. No, it isn't 'peaches and cream' to be a woman in China."

"It doesn't seem exactly a paradise of suffragettes," murmured Ralph.

"No," interjected Tom, "the Government here doesn't have to concern itself about 'hunger strikes' or 'forcible feeding.'"

"To atone to some extent for this hateful feature of family life," said the doctor, "they have another that is altogether admirable, and that is the respect shown to parents. In no country of the world is filial reverence so fully displayed as here. A disobedient son is almost unthinkable, and a murderer would scarcely be regarded with more disapproval. From birth to old age, the son looks upon his father with humility and reverence, and worships him as a god after he is dead. There is nothing of the flippancy with which we are too familiar in our own country. With us the 'child is father of the man,' or, if he isn't, he wants to be. Here the man always remains the father of the child."

"Yes," said Bert, "I remember in Bill Nye's story of his early life he says that at the age of four 'he took his parents by the hand and led them out to Colorado.'"

"And that's no joke," put in the captain. "All the foreigners that visit our country are struck by the independent attitude of children to their parents."

"Another thing we have to place to the credit of this remarkable people," he went on, "is their love for education. The scholar is held in universal esteem. The road to learning is also the road to the highest honors of the State. Every position is filled by competitive examinations, and the one who has the highest mark gets the place. Of course their idea of education is far removed from ours. There is no attempt to develop the power of original thinking, but simply to become familiar with the teaching and wisdom of the past. Still, with all its defects, it stands for the highest that the nation knows, and they crown with laurels the men who rise to the front rank. Of course they wouldn't compare for a moment with the great scholars of the Western world. Still, you know, 'in a nation of the blind, the one-eyed man is king,' and their scholars stand out head and shoulders above the general level, and are reverenced accordingly."

"I suppose that system of theirs explains why the civil service in our own country is slightingly referred to as the 'Chinese' civil service by disgruntled politicians," said Ralph.

"Yes," said the captain, "and speaking of politicians, our Chinese friends could give us cards and spades and beat us out at that game. They're the smoothest and slickest set of grafters in the world. Why, the way they work it here would make our ward politicians turn green with envy. We're only pikers compared with these fellows. Graft is universal all through China. It taints every phase of the national life. Justice is bought and sold like any commodity and with scarcely a trace of shame or concealment. The only concern the mandarin has with the case brought before him is as to which side will make him the richest present. It is a case of the longest purse and little else. Then after a man has been sent to prison, the jailer must be paid to make his punishment as light as possible. If he is condemned to death, the executioner must be paid to do his work as painlessly and quickly as he can. At every turn and corner the grafter stands with his palm held out, and unless you grease it well you might as well abandon your cause at the start. You're certainly foredoomed to failure."

"Well," said Bert, "we're badly enough off at home in the matter of graft, but at least we have some 'chance for our white alley' when we go into a court of justice."

"Yes," assented the doctor, "of course a long purse doesn't hurt there, as everywhere else. But, in the main, our judges are beyond the coarse temptation of money bribes. We've advanced a good deal from the time of Sir Francis Bacon, that 'brightest, wisest, meanest of mankind,' who not only accepted presents from suitors in cases brought before him, but had the nerve to write a pamphlet justifying the practice and claiming that it didn't affect his judgment."

"What do you think of the present revolution in China, doctor?" asked Dick. "Will it bring the people more into sympathy with our way of looking at things?"

He shook his head skeptically.

"No," he answered, "to be frank I don't. Between us and the Chinese there is a great gulf fixed, and I don't believe it will ever be bridged. The Caucasian and Mongolian races are wholly out of sympathy. We look at everything from opposite sides of the shield. We can no more mix than oil and water.

"The white races made a mistake," he went on and the boys detected in his voice a strain of sombre foreboding, "when they drew China out of its shell and forced it to come in contact with the modern world. It was a hermit nation and wanted to remain so. All it asked was to be let alone. It was a sleeping giant. Why did we wake him up unless we wanted to tempt fate and court destruction?

"Not only that, but the giant had forgotten how to fight. We're teaching him how just as fast as we can, and even sending European officers to train and lead his armies. The giant's club was rotten and wormeaten. In its place, we're giving him Gatling guns and rifled artillery, the finest in the world. We have forgotten that Mongol armies have already overrun the world and that they may do it again. We're like the fisherman in the 'Arabian Nights' who found a bottle on the shore and learned that it held a powerful genii. As long as he kept the bottle corked he was safe. But he was foolish enoughto take out the cork, and the genii, escaping, became as big as a mountain, and couldn't be squeezed back into the bottle. We've pulled the cork that held the Chinese genii and we'll never get him back again. Think of four hundred million people, a third of the population of the world, conscious of their strength, equipped with modern arms, trained in the latest tactics, able to live on practically nothing, moving over Europe like a swarm of devastating locusts! When some Chinese Napoleon—and he may be already born—finds such an army at his back—God help Europe!"

He spoke with feeling, and a silence fell upon them as they looked over the great city, and thought of the thousands of miles and countless millions of inhabitants that lay beyond. Did they hear in imagination the gathering of shadowy hosts, the tread of marching armies, and the distant thunder of artillery? Or did they dimly sense with that mysterious clairvoyance sometimes vouchsafed to men that in a few days they themselves would be at death grip with that invisible "yellow peril" and barely win out with their lives?

Dick shivered, though the night was warm.

"Come along, fellows," he said, as the captain and doctor walked away. "Let's go to bed."

CHAPTER XV

THE DRAGON'S CLAWS

The next morning the boys were up bright and early, ready for their trip through the city.

"By George," said Dick, "I have to pinch myself to realize that we're really in China at last. Until a month ago I never dreamed of seeing it. As a matter of course I had hoped and expected to go to Europe and possibly take in Egypt. That seemed the regulation thing to do and it was the limit of my traveling ambition. But as regards Asia, I've never quite gotten over the feeling I had when I was a kid. Then I thought that if I dug a hole through the center of the earth I'd come to China, and, since they were on the under side of the world, I'd find the people walking around upside down."

"Well," laughed Bert, "they're upside down, sure enough, mentally and morally, but physically they don't seem to be having any rush of blood to the head."

An electric launch was at hand, but they preferred to take one of the native sampans that darted in and out among the shipping looking for passengers. They hailed one and it came rapidly to the side.

"See those queer little eyes on each side of the bow," said Tom. "I wonder what they're for?"

"Why, so that the boat can see where it is going," replied Dick. "You wouldn't want it to go it blind and bump head first into the side, would you?"

"And this in a nation that invented the mariner's compass," groaned Tom. "How are the mighty fallen!"

"And even that points to the south in China, while everywhere else it points to the north. Can you beat it?" chimed in Ralph.

"Even their names are contradictions," said Bert. "This place was originally called 'Hiang-Kiang,' 'the place of sweet waters.' But do you catch any whiff here that reminds you of ottar of roses or the perfume wafted from 'Araby the blest?'"

"Well, not so you could notice it," responded Ralph, as the awful smells of the waterside forced themselves on their unwilling nostrils.

They speedily reached the shore and handed double fare to the parchment-faced boatman, who chattered volubly.

"What do you suppose he's saying?" asked Tom.

"Heaven knows," returned Ralph; "thanking us, probably. And yet he may be cursing us as 'foreign devils,' and consigning us to perdition. That's one of the advantages of speaking in the toughest language on earth for an outsider to master."

"It is fierce, isn't it?" assented Bert. "I've heard that it takes about seven years of the hardest kind of study to learn to speak or read it, and even then you can't do it any too well. Some simply can't learn it at all."

"Well," said Tom, "I can't conceive of any worse punishment than to have to listen to it, let alone speak it. Good old United States for mine."

At the outset they found themselves in the English quarter. It was a splendid section of the city, with handsome buildings and well-kept streets, and giving eloquent testimony to the colonizing genius of the British empire. Here England had entrenched herself firmly, and from this as a point of departure, her long arm stretched out to the farthest limits of the Celestial Kingdom. She had made the place a modern Gibraltar, dominating the waters of the East as its older prototype held sway over the Mediterranean. Everywhere there were evidences of the law and order and regulated liberty that always accompany the Union Jack, and that explains why a little island in the Western Ocean rules a larger part of the earth's surface than any other power.

"We've certainly got to hand it to the English," said Ralph. "They're the worst hated nation in Europe, and yet as colonizers the whole world has to take off its hat to them. Look at Egypt and India and Canada and Australia and a score of smaller places. No wonder that Webster was impressed by it when he spoke of the 'drum-beat that, following the sun and keeping pace with the hours, encircled the globe with the martial airs of England.'"

"It's queer, too, why it is so," mused Bert. "If they were specially genial and adaptable, you could understand it. But, as a rule, they're cold and arrogant and distant, and they don't even try to get in touch with the people they rule. Now the French are far more sympathetic and flexible, but, although they have done pretty well in Algiers and Tonquin and Madagascar, they don't compare with the British as colonizers."

"Well," rejoined Ralph, "I suppose the real explanation lies in their tenacity and their sense of justice. They may be hard but they are just, and the people after a while realize that their right to life and property will be protected, and that in their courts the poor have almost an equal chance with the rich. But when all's said and done, I guess we'll simply have to say that they have the genius for colonizing and let it go at that."

"Speaking of justice and fair play, though," said Bert, "there's one big blot on their record, and that is the way they have forced the opium traffic on China. The Chinese as a rule are a temperate race, but there seems to be some deadly attraction for them in opium that they can't resist. It is to them what 'firewater' is to the Indian. The rulers of China realized how it was destroying the nation and tried to prohibit its importation. But England saw a great source of revenue threatened by this reform, as most of the opium comes from the poppy grown in India. So up she comes with her gunboats, this Christian nation, and fairly forces the reluctant rulers to let in the opium under threat of bombardment if they refused. To-day the habit has grown to enormous proportions. It is the curse of China, and the blame for the debauchery of a whole nation lies directly at the door of England and no one else."

By this time they had passed through the British section and found themselves in the native quarter. Here at last they were face to face with the real China. They had practically been in Europe; a moment later and they were in Asia. A new world lay before them.

The streets were very narrow, sometimes not more than eight or ten feet in width. A man standing at a window on one side could leap into one directly opposite. They were winding as well as narrow, and crowded on both sides with tiny shops in which merchants sat beside their wares or artisans plied their trade. Before each shop was a little altar dedicated to the god of wealth, a frank admission that here, as in America, they all worshipped the "Almighty Dollar." Flaunting signs, on which were traced dragons and other fearsome and impossible beasts, hung over the store entrances.

"My," said Ralph, "this would be a bad place for a heavy drinker to find himself in suddenly. He'd think he 'had 'em' sure. Pink giraffes and blue elephants wouldn't be a circumstance to some of these works of art."

"Right you are," assented Tom. "I'll bet if the truth were known the Futurist and Cubist painters, that are making such a splurge in America just now, got their first tips from just such awful specimens as these."

"Well, these narrow streets have one advantage over Fifth Avenue," said Ralph. "No automobile can come along here and propel you into another world."

"No," laughed Bert, "if the 'Gray Ghost' tried to get through here, it would carry away part of the houses on each side of the street. The worst thing that can run over us here is a wheelbarrow."

"Or a sedan chair," added Tom, as one of these, bearing a passenger, carried by four stalwart coolies, brushed against him.

A constant din filled the air as customers bargained with the shop-keepers over the really beautiful wares displayed on every hand. Rare silks and ivories and lacquered objects were heaped in rich profusion in the front of the narrow stalls, and their evident value stood out in marked contrast to the squalid surroundings that served as a setting.

"No 'one price' here, I imagine," said Ralph, as the boys watched the noisy disputes between buyer and seller.

"No," said Bert. "To use a phrase that our financiers in America are fond of, they put on 'all that the traffic will bear.' I suppose if you actually gave them what they first asked they'd throw a fit or drop dead. I'd hate to take the chance."

"It would be an awful loss, wouldn't it?" asked Tom sarcastically, as he looked about at the immense crowd swarming like bees from a hive. "Where could they find anyone to take his place?"

"There are quite a few, aren't there?" said Ralph. "The mystery is where they all live and sleep. There don't seem to be enough houses in the town to take care of them all."

"No," remarked Bert, "but what the town lacks in the way of accommodations is supplied by the river. Millions of the Chinese live in the boats along the rivers, and at night you can see them pouring down to the waterside in droves. A white man needs a space six feet by two when he's dead, but a Chinaman doesn't need much more than that while he is alive. A sardine has nothing on him when it comes to saving space and packing close."

At every turn their eyes were greeted with something new and strange. Here a wandering barber squatted in the street and carried on his trade as calmly as though in a shop of his own. Tinkers mended pans, soothsayers told fortunes, jugglers and acrobats held forth to delighted crowds, snake charmers put their slimy pets through a bewildering variety of exhibitions. Groups of idlers played fan-tan and other games of chance, and through the waving curtains of queerly painted booths came at times the acrid fumes of opium. Mingled with these were the odors of cooking, some repellant and some appetizing, which latter reminded the boys that it was getting toward noon and their healthy appetites began to assert themselves. They looked at each other.

"Well," said Ralph, "how about the eats?"

"I move that we have some," answered Tom.

"Second the motion," chimed in Dick.

"Carried unanimously," added Bert, "but where?"

"Perhaps we would better get back to the English quarter," suggested Ralph. "There are some restaurants there as good as you can find in New York or London."

"Not for mine," said Tom. "We can do that at any time, but it isn't often we'll have a chance to eat in a regular Chinese restaurant. Let's take our courage in our hands and go into the next one here we come to. It's all in a lifetime. Come along."

"Tom's right," said Dick. "Let's shut our eyes and wade in. It won't kill us, and we'll have one more experience to look back upon. So 'lead on, MacDuff.'"

Accordingly they all piled into the next queer little eating-house they came to, but not before they had agreed among themselves that they would take the whole course from "soup to nuts," no matter what their stomachs or their noses warned them against. A suave, smiling Chinaman seated them with many profound bows at a quaint table, on which were the most delicate of plates and the most tiny and fragile of cups. They had of course to depend on signs, but they made him understand that they wanted a full course dinner, and that they left the choice of the food to him. They had no cause to regret this, for, despite their misgivings, the dinner was surprisingly good. The shark-fin soup was declared by Ralph to be equal to terrapin. They fought a little shy of indulging heartily in the meat, especially after Bert had mischievously given a tiny squeak that made Tom turn a trifle pale; but in the main they stuck manfully to their pledge, and, to show that they were no "pikers" but "game sports," tasted at least something of each ingredient set before them. And when they came to the dessert, they gave full rein to their appetites, for it was delicious. Candied fruits and raisins and nuts were topped off with little cups of the finest tea that the boys had ever tasted. They paid their bill and left the place with a much greater respect for Chinese cookery than they had ever expected to entertain.

The afternoon slipped away as if by magic in these new and fascinating surroundings. They wove in and out among the countless shops, picking up souvenirs here and there, until their pockets were much heavier and their purses correspondingly lighter. Articles were secured for a song that would have cost them ten times as much in any American city, if indeed they could be bought at all. The ivory carvers, workers in jade, silk dealers, painters of rice-paper pictures, porcelain and silver sellers—all these were many cash richer by the time the boys, tired but delighted, turned back to the shore and were conveyed to the Fearless.

"Well," smiled the doctor, as they came up the side, "how did you enjoy your first day ashore in China?"

"Simply great," responded Bert, enthusiastically, while the others concurred. "I never had so many new sensations crowding upon me at one time in all my whole life before. As a matter of fact I'm bewildered by it yet. I suppose it will be some days before I can digest it and have a clear recollection of all we've seen and done to-day."

"Yes," said the doctor, "but, even yet, you haven't seen the real China. Hong-Kong is so largely English that even the native quarter is more or less influenced by it. Now, Canton is Chinese through and through. Although of course there are foreign residents there, they form so small a part of the population that they are practically nil. It's only about seventy miles away, and I'm going down there to-morrow on a little business of my own. How would you fellows like to come along? Provided, of course, that the captain agrees."

Needless to say the boys agreed with a shout, and the consent of the captain was readily obtained.

"How shall we go?" asked Ralph.

"What's the matter with taking the 'Gray Ghost' along?" put in Tom.

The doctor shook his head.

"No," said he. "That would be all right if the roads were good. Of course they're fine here in the city and for a few miles out. But beyond that they're simply horrible. If it should be rainy you'd be mired to the hubs, and even if the weather keeps dry, the roads in places are mere footpaths. They weren't constructed with a view to automobile riding."

So they took an English river steamer the next day, and before night reached the teeming city, full of color and picturesque to a degree not attained by any other coast city of the Empire. Their time was limited and there was so much to see that they scarcely knew where to begin. But here again the vast experience of the doctor stood them in good stead. Under his expert guidance next day they visited the Tartar City, the Gate of Virtue, the Flowery Pagoda, the Clepsydra or Water Clock, the Viceroy's Yamen, the City of the Dead, and the Temple of the Five Hundred Genii. The latter was a kind of Chinese "Hall of Fame," with images of the most famous statesmen, soldiers, scholars, and philosophers that the country had produced. Before their shrines fires were kept constantly burning, and the place was heavy with the pungent odor of joss sticks and incense.

They wound up with a visit to the execution ground and the prisons, a vivid reminder of the barbarism that foreign influence has as yet not been able to modify to any great degree. The boys were horrified at the devilish ingenuity displayed by the Chinese in their system of punishment.

Here was a poor fellow condemned to the torture of the cangue. This was a species of treebox built about him with an opening at the neck through which his head protruded. He stood upon a number of thin slabs of wood. Every day one of these was removed so that his weight rested more heavily on the collar surrounding his neck, until finally his toes failed to touch the wood at the bottom and he hung by the neck until he slowly strangled to death.

"Yes," said the doctor, as the boys turned away sickened by the sight, "there is no nation so cruel and unfeeling as the Chinese. Scarcely one of these that pass by indifferently, would save this poor fellow if they could. They look unmoved on scenes that would freeze the blood in our veins."

"This is bad enough," he went on, "but it is nothing to some of the fiendish atrocities that they indulge in. Their executioners could give points on torture to a Sioux Indian.

"They have for instance what they call the 'death of the thousand slices.' They are such expert anatomists that they can carve a man continuously for hours without touching a vital spot. They hang the victim on a kind of cross and cut slices from every part of his body before death comes to his relief.

"Then, too, they have what they name the 'vest of death.' They strip a man to the waist and put on him a coat of mail with numberless fine openings. They pull this tightly about him until the flesh protrudes through the open places, and then deftly pass a razor all over it, making a thousand tiny wounds. Then they take off the vest and release the victim. The many wounds coalesce in one until he is practically flayed and dies in horrible torment."

The boys shuddered at these instances of "man's inhumanity to man."

"Life must be horribly cheap in China," observed Tom.

"I wonder if such terrible punishment really has any effect as an example to criminals," said Ralph.

"I don't believe it does," put in Bert. "We know that formerly in Europe there were hundreds of crimes that were punishable with death. In England, at one time, a young boy or girl would be hung for stealing a few shillings. And yet crime grew more common as punishment grew more severe. When they became more humane in dealing with offenders, the number of crimes fell off in proportion."

"Yes," assented the doctor. "The modern idea is right that punishment should be reformatory instead of vindictive. But it will be a good while before China sees things from that standpoint."

"It is possible of course that the culprit here does not suffer so cruelly as a white man would under similar conditions. The nervous system of a Chinaman is very coarse and undeveloped. He bears with stolidity torture that would wring shrieks of agony from one more highly strung."

"Perhaps so," said Bert, "but I don't know. We say that sometimes about fish. They're coldblooded, and so it doesn't hurt them to be caught. I've often thought, though, that it would be interesting if we could hear from the fish on that point."

"No doubt," returned the doctor. "It's always easy to be philosophical when somebody else is concerned. But we'll have to go now," looking at his watch, "if we expect to get to the boat in time."

"Well, fellows," said Bert that night as, safe on board of the Fearless, they prepared to tumble in, "it certainly is interesting to go about this land of the 'Yellow Dragon,' but it's a cruel old beast. I'd hate to feel its teeth and claws."

Was it a touch of prophecy?

CHAPTER XVI

THE PIRATE ATTACK

"Not very pretty to look at, is he?" asked Ralph, indicating by a nod the huge Chinaman who had slipped noiselessly past them on his way to the galley.

"He isn't exactly a beauty," assented Tom, looking after the retreating figure, "but then what Chinaman is? Besides he didn't sign as an Adonis, but as an assistant cook. What do you expect to get for your twelve dollars a month and found?"

"Well, I'd hate to meet him up an alley on a dark night, especially if he had a knife," persisted Ralph. "If ever villainy looked out from a fellow's face it does from his."

"Don't wake him up, he is dreaming," laughed Bert.

"I do not like thee, Doctor Fell,The reason why I cannot tell;But this one thing I know full well,I do not like thee, Doctor Fell,"

quoted Dick.

"Come out of your trance, Ralph, and look at these two junks just coming out from that point of land over there," rallied Tom. "Those fellows handle them smartly, don't they?"

It was a glorious evening off the China coast. The Fearless had hoisted anchor and turned her prow toward home. Every revolution of the screws was bringing them nearer to the land of the Stars and Stripes. The sea was like quicksilver, there was a following wind, the powerful engines were moving like clockwork, and everything indicated a fast and prosperous voyage.

The boys were gathered at the rail, and, as Tom spoke, they gazed with interest at the two long narrow junks that were drawing swiftly toward them. All sails were set and they slipped with surprising celerity through the water.

"They both seem to be going in the same direction," said Ralph. "It almost looks as though they were racing. I'll bet on the—What was that?"

The ship shook from stem to stern as though her machinery had been suddenly thrown out of place.

The captain rushed down from the bridge and the mates came running forward. The boys had leaped to their feet and looked at each other in dismay. Then, with one accord, they plunged down in the direction of the engine-room. Before they reached it they could hear the hoarse shouts of MacGregor and his assistants as they shut off the steam, and the ship losing headway tossed helplessly up and down.

"What is it Mr. MacGregor?" asked the captain.

"I canna' tell yet," answered Mac. "Something must have dropped into the machinery. And yet I'll swear there was nothing lying around loose. But I'll find out."

A minute or two passed and then with a snarl and an oath, he held up a heavy wrench.

"Here's the thing that did it," he yelled, "and it didn't get there by accident either. I ken every tool aboard this ship and I never set eyes on this before. Somebody threw it there to wreck the engines."

"To wreck the engines," repeated Captain Manning. "Why? Who'd want to do anything like that?"

"I dinna' ken," said Mac stubbornly. "I only know some one must ha'. I'd like to get these twa hands of mine on his throat."

"Has any one been here except you and your men?" asked the captain.

"No one—leastwise nane but the Chink. He stopped to say ——"

Bert jumped as though he had been shot. The Chinaman of the villainous face—those junks putting out from land! Like a flash he was up the ladder and out on the deserted deck. His heart stood still as he looked astern.

The two junks were seething with activity and excitement. The decks were packed with men. All pretense of secrecy was abandoned. The stopping of the ship had evidently been the signal they were expecting. All sails were bent to catch every breath of air, and long sweeps darted suddenly from the sides. The prows threw up fountains of water on each side as the junks made for the crippled ship like wolves leaping on the flanks of a wounded deer.

Bert took this in at a single glance. He saw it all—the Chinese accomplice, the carefully prepared plan, the wrecking of the machinery. His voice rang out like a trumpet:

"Pirates! Pirates! All hands on deck!"

Then, while the officers and crew came tumbling up from below, he rushed to the wireless room and pressed the spark key. The blue flames sputtered, as up and down the China coast and far out to sea his message flashed:

"Attacked by pirates. Help. Quick."

Then followed the latitude and longitude. He could not wait for a reply. Three times at intervals of a few seconds he sent the call, and then he sprang from his seat.

"Here, Howland," he shouted, as his assistant appeared at the door. "Keep sending right along. It's a matter of life and death. Let me know if an answer comes."

Then he grabbed his .45 and rushed on deck. A fight was coming—a fight against fearful odds. And his blood grew hot with the lust of battle.

Short sharp words of command ran over the ship. The officers and crew were at their places. The women passengers had been sent below and an incipient panic had been quelled at the start. The officers had their revolvers loaded and ready and the crew were armed with capstan bars and marlinspikes beside the sheath knives that they all carried. There was no cannon, except a small signal gun on board the ship, and this the pirates knew. The battle must be hand to hand. The odds were heavy. The decks of the enemy swarmed with yelling devils naked to the waist and armed to the teeth. They were at least five to one and had the advantage of the attack and the surprise.

The boys were grouped together at the stern toward which the junks were pulling. All had revolvers, and heavy bars lay near by to be grabbed when they should come to hand-grips with the pirates. They looked into each others eyes and each rejoiced at what he saw there. Together they had faced death before and won out; to-day, they were facing it again, and the chances were against their winning. Yet they never quailed or flinched. The spirit of '76 was there—the spirit of 1812—the spirit of '61. They came of a fighting stock; a race that could face and whip the world or die in the trying. They glanced at Old Glory floating serenely above their heads, and each swore to himself that if he died defeated he would not die disgraced. Their fingers tightened on the butts of their weapons, their teeth clinched and their eyes grew hard.

The captain, cool and stern, as he always was in a crisis, had divided his forces into two equal parts. He himself commanded on the port side, while Mr. Collins took charge of the starboard. A long line of hose had been connected with the boiling water of the engine room, and two sailors held the nozzle as it writhed and twisted on the rail. Had there been but one junk, this might have proved decisive, but, in the nature of things, it could only defend one side of the ship. The pirates were proceeding on the plan of "divide and conquer." As they drew rapidly nearer, they separated, and while one dashed at the port side of the ship, the other swept around under the starboard quarter. Then a horde of half-naked yellow fiends with knives held between their teeth swarmed up the sides, grabbed at the rails and sought to obtain a foothold. A volley of bullets swept the first of them away, but their places were instantly taken by others. The boiling water rushed in a torrent over the port side, and the scalded scoundrels fell back. But it was only for a moment and still they kept coming with unabated fury.

Bert and his comrades fought shoulder to shoulder. Their revolvers barked again and again and the snarling yellow faces were so near that they could not miss. Many fell back dead and wounded, but they never quit; and when the revolvers were emptied, a number of the pirates got over the rail, while the boys were reloading. Then followed a savage hand-to-hand fight. Iron bars came down with sickening crashes; knives flashed and fell and rose and fell again. The pirates were gaining a foothold and the little band of defenders was hard pressed. But just then reinforcements came in the form of MacGregor and his husky stokers and engineers. They had been trying desperately to repair the engines, but the sounds of the fight above had been too much for them to stand, and now they came headlong into the fight, their brawny arms swinging iron bars like flails. They turned the tide at that critical moment and the pirates were driven back over the sides. They dropped sullenly into the junks and drew away from the ship until they were out of range of bullets. Then they stopped and took breath before renewing the attack. They had suffered terribly, but they still vastly outnumbered the defenders.

The boys reloaded their revolvers, watching the enemy narrowly.

"I wonder if they have enough," said Dick as he bound a handkerchief around a slight flesh wound in his left arm.

"I don't think so," answered Bert, "their blood is up and they know how few we are as compared with themselves. They certainly fought like wildcats."

"They're live wires sure enough," agreed Tom. "They—why Bert, what's the matter?" he exclaimed as Bert sprang to his feet excitedly.

But Bert had rushed to the captain and was eagerly laying before him the plan that Tom's words had unwittingly suggested.

The captain listened intently and an immense relief spread over his features. He issued his orders promptly. Great coils of heavy wire were brought from the storeroom and under Bert's supervision were wound in parallel rows about the stern of the ship. At first sight it looked as though they were inviting the pirates to grasp them and thus easily reach the deck. It seemed like committing suicide. The work was carried on with feverish energy and by the time the pirates swung their boats around and again headed for the ship, there was a treble row of wires about a foot apart on both the port and starboard side.

The revolvers had all been reloaded and every man stood ready. But the tenseness of a few minutes before was lacking. For the first time since the fight began Captain Manning smiled contentedly.

"Don't fire, men, unless I give the word. Stand well back from the rail and wait for orders."

On came the pirates yelling exultantly. The silence of the defenders was so strange and unnatural that it might well have daunted a more imaginative or less determined foe. Not a shot was fired, not a man stirred. They might have been dream men on a dream ship for any sign of life and movement. The crowded junks bore down on either side of the ship, and as though with a single movement, a score of pirates leaped at the rails and grasped the wires to pull themselves aboard.

Then a wonderful thing happened. From below came the buzz of the great dynamo and through the wires surged the tremendous power of the electric current. It was appalling, overwhelming, irresistible. It killed as lightning kills. There was not even time for a cry. They hung there for one awful moment with limbs twisted and contorted, while an odor of burning flesh filled the air. Then they dropped into the sea. Their comrades petrified with horror saw them fall and then with frantic shrieks bent to the sweeps and fled for their lives.

And so it befell that when the good ship Fearless drew up to the dock at San Francisco, the young wireless operator, much to his surprise as well as distaste, found that his quick wit and unfailing courage had made of him a popular hero. But he steadfastly disclaimed having done anything unusual.

If he had fought a good fight and "kept the faith," it was, after all, only his duty.

"Well, yes, but admitting all that," said Dick, "it's so unusual for a fellow to do even that, that when it does happen the world insists on crowning it. You know.

"'The path of duty is the road to glory.'"

Neither knew at the moment how much of prophecy there was in that quotation. For Glory beckoned, though unseen, and Bert in the near future was destined to win fresh laurels. How gallantly he fought for them, how splendidly he won them and how gracefully he wore them will be told in

"Bert Wilson, Marathon Winner."

THE END